A SPARK to the PAST

By Cynthia Wall, KA7ITT

Cover and illustrations by Sheila Dianne Somerville

DIMI PRESS
3820 Oak Hollow Lane, SE
Salem, Oregon 97302-4774
© 1998 by Cynthia Wall, KA7ITT

ISBN: 0-931625-34-3

Printed in the United States of America

Library of Congress Catalog Card Number: 98-96034

Cover and illustrations by Sheila Dianne Somerville
Typeface 12 pt. Palatino
Printing by Gilliland Printing, Arkansas City, Kansas

"There are more things in heaven and earth, Horatio,
Than are dreamt of in your philosophy."

Hamlet. William Shakespeare

Also by Cynthia Wall

NIGHT SIGNALS

HOSTAGE IN THE WOODS

FIREWATCH!

EASY TARGET

DISAPPEARING ACT

For the Students of Waldo Middle
School
Salem, Oregon

Thanks for sharing the adventure.

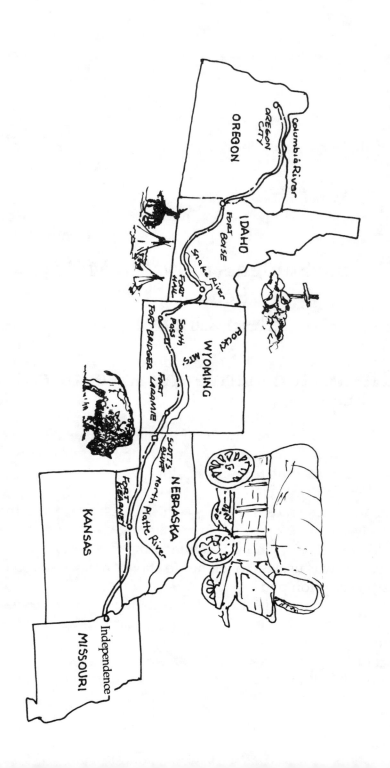

Chapter 1

An Electrifying Meeting

"Open wide."

Kim stretched her mouth open as Dr. Harrison peered into her throat with a flashlight and wiped a swab against the red tissues.

"How long has it been sore?"

"Two days."

"Hmmm."

The white-haired doctor who had taken care of her since birth wiped the swab on a slide.

"I'll send this to the lab. There's a lot of strep going around so I want you to call first thing in the morning to see if we need to start you on antibiotics."

"Oh, Dr. Harrison, I won't be here in the morning. Marc and I are giving a demonstration at the ham radio club tonight and then some of us are going up near Marion Forks for a week-end search and rescue training session."

Dr. Harrison smiled.

"You and those radios. I suppose it's useless to tell you that with a fever you ought to be staying home."

He looked at Kim who was telling him with her expression that, 'yes,' it was useless to tell her to stay home. He scribbled on his prescription pad.

"This is for Penicillin. Go ahead and take it over the week-end and call me on Monday and we'll see if you need to take the full course."

"I could call you tomorrow through a phone patch."

"Good. I won't be here, but the nurse will have the results. If the culture's negative, stop taking the pills. If it's positive, keep on."

"Thank you Dr. Harrison."

Kim gathered up her backpack and started for the door.

"One more thing, Kim."

"Yes?"

"Strep is quite contagious. I wouldn't go kissing that young man of yours until the test comes back."

"Okay, I'll tell him doctor's orders."

Kim smiled as she left his office.

****

When she told Marc about the tentative diagnosis on the way to the club meeting, he was quite concerned.

"Strep is nothing to mess around with. Are you sure you should be going on the campout with midterms next week?"

"I don't even know if that's what it is, and besides I'm already started on medication. I'll be fine," she reassured him.

She looked over at the tall, slender, dark-haired college student beside her. Although they had known each other for over a year, she still felt her heart jump a beat every time she saw him.

Marc peered with disgust at the rain splattering the windshield.

"I was hoping to try out my new solar charger this weekend," he said.

"The last weather I heard said snow down to 4500 feet."

"And it's not even Halloween," Marc said. " So much for El Niño."

He pulled his car into the parking lot of the high school where the Salem Amateur Radio Club held its monthly meetings and Kim and Marc unloaded the Spark Gap transmitter that was to be the demonstration that night. The Spark Gap or "Sparky" as Marc affectionately called it had belonged to his grandfather and had once been demonstrated at the 1906 World's Fair by his great grandfather. Most of the people attending tonight had never seen one, and Marc was looking forward to showing it off.

"Technology has definitely lightened the load," Marc laughed as he carried in the heavy black box.

"Whatcha got? Whatcha got?" five year old Bobby Courson asked, running in circles around Marc and Kim as they walked down the hall into the gym where the meetings were held.

"A secret," Kim whispered to him. "It's a magical box."

"Really? Like what? Turn us into monsters?"

"Wait and see," Kim told him.

Bobby put his hand out to touch the Spark Gap as Marc set it gently on the table in the front of the gym. A group of club members gathered around as Marc checked the various wires and connections.

"It's magic and I'm going to help," Bobby announced. His father ruffled his hair and smiled. Bobby could be a handful. He didn't seem to be able to sit still and he asked questions constantly, but everyone tried hard to answer them patiently.

Kim and Marc set their backpacks by the table and then went to get the rest of their demonstration from Marc's car. What they planned to do was show how the earliest radio transmissions were made between a Spark Gap and a "Coherer" – a glass cylinder with carbon filings that joined or "cohered" when an electrical impulse was received. In tonight's demo, the joined filings would open a relay, sounding a bell clapper inside the dome. Spark Gap demonstrations were always noisy, sparky, and lots of fun.

During the brief business meeting, Kim tried not to think about her sore throat and a headache that was gaining in intensity. She hoped that by the time Marc picked her up tomorrow at 5 a.m. for the drive to the survival camp that she would be feeling better. She looked at her backpack lying under the demo table and made a mental note to add some aspirin and cough drops when she got home.

Club President, Ron Mathis, was always a character. He held up a brown paper bag tied with a red ribbon.

"How many are going tomorrow?"

Ten people raised their hands.

3

"Okay, one by one, I want you to come up here and show the contents of your survival packs. We'll take a vote as to who's the best prepared and the winner will get this fantastic prize personally selected by yours truly. I guarantee it's something that will come in handy at the survival camp."

"Probably a Big Mac and fries," someone in the front row chuckled.

When it was Kim's turn, she walked to the front of the room and spread out the contents of her back pack. Change of clothes, survival foods, first aid supplies, 2 meter transmitter, battery pack, canteen, sterno, matches, wilderness maps, compass, knife, collapsible camp shovel, and sleeping bag. She didn't mention the Penicillin as that was in her pocket.

Some of the others had packs so heavy, she wondered how they'd be able to carry them, but the prize winner was Marc. Once badly injured in the woods, he didn't take anything for granted. Not only did he carry a two meter rig with battery packs and a solar charger, he also had his HW-9, a home-built radio that had once saved his life, along with extra antenna and ground line. Thermal underwear, a survival blanket, instant heat packs: it looked like he was planning a trip to the Arctic. Surprisingly, his pack only weighed 37 pounds.

"I cut out a lot of the food," he told the club president as he accepted his prize. "I found that if you just have water, you can do without food for quite a few days."

"Well this will come in extra handy," said Ron as he handed him the brown paper bag.

Marc opened it and reached in to pull out a fistful of chocolate candy bars which brought a laugh from the members. Marc started to put the candy bars in his backpack but then reached over and dumped them all into Kim's.

"She's the one who's the chocaholic."

"Oh yeah, I'm sure you won't eat any," Kim laughed.

There was a brief intermission for coffee, cookies, and conversation, and then Kim and Marc took center stage. Bobby Courson sat in the front row, his eyes glued on the Spark Gap transmitter.

Everyone listened as Marc gave a brief history of Spark Gap transmitters including the one that sent the SOS from the Titanic. While he talked, Kim set the Coherer on a table across the room and made sure the transmitter was plugged into the extension cord stretched to the front of the gym.

"I never met my great-grandfather," Marc said, "but I know he thought this was a wonderful invention. It's too bad he couldn't have lived long enough to see where we are now in technology."

Marc reached over for a final inspection of all the wires and connections. Kim walked to stand by him.

"Okay, I think we're just about ready to turn it on. Oops, wait a minute," Marc said, leaning forward to fiddle with a connection. His foot caught in one of the straps of their backpacks piled under the table and he tried to kick it loose.

Kim reached down to move the packs to the side, but just as she grabbed the straps, Kim saw Bobby Courson get out of his chair and move up beside Marc.

"I want to turn it on," the five year old said, his hand reaching toward the switch.

"No!" Kim and Marc yelled simultaneously.

There was a huge flash and then blackness. Somewhere in the distance, Kim heard a bell ringing and loud thunder claps. Her head hurt and she closed her eyes tightly against the bright light that seemed to be filling her head with sparks.

Chapter 2

Struck by Lightning

E mil Burchart saw it first. A shard of light that stitched the clouds together in a blanket of white.
"Take cover!" he yelled.

People all over the camp dived under and into the wagons as lightning incinerated a dry shrub at the edge of the clearing. A fraction of a second later, thunder exploded, sending shock waves into the ground. Cowering under the Malby's wagon with his wife, Adeline, Emil pressed his hands over his ears, trying to block the percussive blasts of sound. There was a second bright light and the hair on the back of his neck stood up from the tremendous static electricity. Even before he turned his head to look, Emil just knew the lightning was going to strike his own wagon, parked at the far edge of the group.

Squinting his eyes against the terrible brightness, he craned his neck, trying to glimpse their wagon. His mouth dropped open in horror — Kimberly and Marcus and Robert were running across the clearing. They reached the Burchart wagon and Marcus tried to boost young Robert up over the edge when suddenly, the three of them were encapsulated in whiteness. Emil watched as Kimberly's arms flailed out to her sides and Marcus dropped to his knees, trying to shield Robert with his body. The smell of burnt cloth and smoldering wood penetrated the air. Ignoring the danger to himself, Emil squeezed out from his protective cover and ran to the lifeless forms on the ground.

****

"Marc?" Kim moaned without opening her eyes.

An enormous growl of thunder rumbled overhead; brilliant lightning flashes penetrated her closed eyes. Funny... she didn't remember there being a thunderstorm.

"Oh," she groaned again, raising a tingling hand to her throbbing head.

A gruff man's voice broke through the dark haze.

"Don't anybody touch them. They're electrified."

Kim's eyes snapped open. An older man and woman dressed in pioneer costumes were standing a few feet away watching her with wary concern. The air was thick with smoke and directly in front of her were the charred remains of some wooden structure.

"Kim?"

Kim raised her head to see Marc sitting up on the ground beside her, rubbing his head. Little Bobby lay on the ground next to them, whimpering.

"What happened?" she asked weakly.

"I don't know," Marc said, looking up dazed at the crowd of people, all dressed in costume, gathering around them.

"You all got struck by lightning; that's what," said Emil. "You folks all right?"

"I think so," Marc said, still rubbing his head. "Who are you?"

Another man, tall and thin with a long beard, reached out and quickly touched Marc on the shoulder. He pulled back his finger and announced: "It's okay. The fire's all gone out of them. They're just a little touched in the head, that's all."

Kim sat up and looked around her. *Where were they? Where were the club members and who were these strange people?*

The man who had touched Marc, apparently the bold one of the group, reached a cane up and tapped the burnt circular frame above them.

"You're blessed, Emil. I don't think it burned through the structure none. Just singed the canvas and wood."

"What?" Marc said.

"I want my mommie," Bobby sobbed, sitting up, clutching his head between his hands.

Now, the older woman moved in and put a comforting arm around Bobby.

"Of course you do, Robert. We all miss your dear Mama and your father, too," the woman said to him. She looked over at Kim and Marc. "Thanks be the three of you survived that firestorm. Praise the Lord for that. You rest a little and you'll be fine."

Kim looked at the woman. *Who was she? And why was she talking to them?* Bobby, crying loudly, covered his eyes and then uncovered them again as if he hoped what he was seeing would go away. Kim's eyes went back and forth from him to the woman. Bobby was dressed in dusty, dark woolen clothes. He looked over at Kim in bewilderment.

Kim stared down at her legs and shook her head. *What on earth was going on?* She was dressed in the same outlandish costume that the others were. She squinted her eyes and turned to Marc. *Oh my.* He could have stepped right out of the 1800's, wide-brimmed leather hat and beard and all. She closed her eyes. What a strange dream she was having.

"There's hot porridge ready for you by the fire. That's all there is for supper tonight, so as soon as you feel able, I'd get to it. I think the storm's about over."

With that, the woman gathered up her skirts and walked toward a group of women gathered around a campfire. Kim and Bobby and Marc sat in a daze, watching the rain turn to mist.

"Kim?" Bobby whimpered.

"Are you okay, Bobby?"

The little boy crawled over to her and snuggled into her arms. Kim looked again at the long, dusty dress she was wearing. Were those her arms sticking out of the sleeves? They looked so thin. She wiggled her fingers and felt a rumble of hunger in her stomach that seemed strange and familiar at the same time. She shook her head, trying to clear her thoughts.

"Where are we?"

"This can't be," Marc said quietly.

"What are you thinking?"

He didn't have time to answer Kim's question because another man, closer to his age, came over just then.

"Can you stand up, Marcus?"

Marc struggled to his feet.

"You certainly gave us a scare there. I wish you could rest but Benjamin needs us both to help with that broken wheel."

He took Marc by the arm as though he might need support and led him toward another wagon. Marc gave a bewildered glance back at Kim and then disappeared into the group.

Kim made a closer assessment of Bobby. He was just as dirty and thin appearing as she was. Deep circles shadowed his blue eyes and he was crying... crying hard. Kim felt a sudden urge to join him, but she swallowed hard and took the little boy by the hand.

"Hurry on up, now."

The older woman was back, urging them toward the campfire where they sat down on flat rocks and watched the flames reflect off the faces of the dozen or so women doing chores around its edge. The woman placed steaming bowls of porridge in their hands. Kim looked down at hers and shook her head, trying to clear it.

"Eat it before it cools off," the woman told them.

Kim felt her stomach leap in hunger at the smell of the cereal and without thinking, she began spooning it into her mouth. Bobby was still whimpering.

"I want some milk and sugar," he said between sniffles.

Another woman laughed.

"That lightning did change those two in the head, Adeline."

The kind-faced woman, who Kim gathered was Adeline, sat down beside Bobby and spoke softly.

"Robert, child, don't you remember that Bessie died two months ago and we lost the sugar barrels in the Platte River? You'll have to eat your porridge plain."

9

Adeline's Diary

October 21, 1845

Dear Diary:

Kimberly and Robert are finally eating so I will use this time alone to tell you of the day's events. The sun has just set on the most amazing event I have ever witnessed. Lightning came into our camp and struck three of our people. The miracle is that they are alive. They may have some lingering effects as I noticed they were staggering when they walked to the fire. Kimberly said she had a terrible headache with bright lights going off in her head. Little Robert seemed terribly confused, but they are young and strong and I know in my heart that they will be fine. We are just grateful they are still alive. My spirit is surely sore from all the dear friends we have buried along the trail, and if we had lost those young people, it would be another great sadness.

I was used to the thunder and lightning storms we had back in Missouri, but I have never seen the likes of the one that invaded our camp tonight. It came out of nowhere and struck like the Devil. We are all so fortunate that no worse calamity befell us. Our wagon was the only one that caught fire at all, and it doesn't seem to have hurt it much. All the animals were spared, and I pray that in a day or so Kimberly and Marcus and Robert will be back to their normal selves.

Chapter 3

The Past Becomes the Present

W*here are we?* Kim thought as she desperately tried to visualize an Oregon map in her mind.

But am I even in Oregon? she wondered. She shivered as a gust of cool wind swept through the camp, fanning the fire. Women around the clearing grabbed shawls to put around them. Their thin, grim faces seemed to be filled with despair as they glanced at the thick clouds scudding across the new moon. A couple of them set to the task of pouring rainwater from collecting pans into jugs.

Kim gobbled the lumpy, tasteless porridge, grateful for the warmth it made in her stomach. And, after a few gagging sounds, Bobby ate his too. The women seemed to be oblivious to Kim and Bobby as though it was just everyday that two strangers popped in. Kim looked over at a young woman about her age who was quite pregnant. She was sitting on a log knitting some little booties by the firelight. She looked up at Kim.

"I'm glad you're okay."

"Thank you," Kim said.

"It would have been a real tragedy if God had taken you before your wedding."

The woman sighed and rubbed her hand over her round belly. Her face, like that of all the women, was tired and thin. Kim listened to her, too confused to ask questions.

"I wish my Jack hadn't insisted on us getting married last year before we left Missouri. I should have known better," she said rubbing her stomach again. "Looks like this baby is going to be born on the trail."

Getting married? Kim swallowed hard.

"Kim and me got zapped with a big flash of 'lectricity," Bobby said.

The young woman smiled at him.

"Yes, I know," the woman said. "We all saw it. That's called lightning," she said in an explaining tone.

"I mean before that," Bobby answered, annoyed.

"Oh Robert, you and your tales. You sound like Marcus – always talking about electricity and inventions. Next thing we know, you'll be wanting to fly to the moon."

Bobby's mouth dropped open as he stared at Kim who gave him a warning "no" shake of her head.

"Hannah, come help me clean out this wagon,"an older woman in a long brown dress with a soiled white apron called from the rear of the wagon next to Kim's.

Hannah pushed herself up from the log with difficulty and walked the slow waddling gait of the very pregnant over to the wagon.

"Why'd she say that about the moon?" Bobby whispered to Kim.

Kim cupped his face in her hands.

"Listen, Bobby. I don't know what happened to us. Either we're asleep and dreaming or somehow that spark gap transmitter – the one you turned on while Marc was still touching it – somehow sent us back in time. I know it sounds crazy, but it's the only thing I can think of."

Bobby's lower lip quivered.

"Will I ever see my mommie again?"

Kim felt her own eyes fill with tears.

"I hope so, Bobby. I hope so. I want to see my parents too. But for now, let's not tell these people where we came from and about space travel and all the stuff that happens every day."

"Why not?"

"People… people sometimes don't like people who are different."

Bobby looked down at his feet clad in leather boots so worn the soles were hanging loose.

"We're not different. These are yucky clothes, but we're not different."

"I know, but the things we know are different. You're too young to know much about history, but I think we're somewhere over 100 years ago. And people back then didn't know about space shuttles and moon landings."

"Or Luke Skywalker or Hans Solo or Power Rangers?"

"No, none of that."

"We should tell them. They'd like them."

"Not yet, Bobby. I think it might scare them, and if what we know about scared them, they might be scared of us."

Bobby's eyes, still full of tears, showed that he didn't understand that concept. Kim put her arm around him.

"Let's just be quiet and see if we can figure out where and when we are, okay?"

Bobby nodded.

"Where's Marc?"he asked.

"He went to help someone, I think."

"Are you getting married?" he asked solemnly. "That lady said you were getting married."

"I don't know that either, Bobby."

"I don't like this porridge stuff, " he said putting his bowl on the ground. "I want some Cocoa Crispies."

The older woman from their wagon came back over.

"Go wash your bowl, Robert. You know how to do that. No reason men folk can't help too, isn't that right, Kimberly?"

"Oh absolutely," Kim said weakly.

She stood up and picked up her own bowl and walked with Bobby in the general direction the woman had pointed. Sure enough, there was a pan of hot water sitting on a log with some muslin cloths lying nearby. Kim and Bobby washed their bowls and dried them and stacked them in a wooden box next to others.

"Time for bed now," Adeline told them. "You two have had enough excitement for one day."

With her head still throbbing, Kim followed the old woman back to the charred wagon. Adeline gestured toward a cleared area inside between rows of stacked barrels and farm tools. Kim climbed in over the edge and helped Bobby in behind her. Adeline stood at the end watching as the two covered themselves up with quilts. Kim lay down on the hard floor, her mind filled with thoughts, but before any of them could take form completely, she fell asleep.

The next thing she knew Bobby was shaking her awake.

"We're still here," he said plaintively. "Where's my mommie?"

Kim sat up and rubbed her eyes. She looked down at her worn, dirty dress. If this was a dream, it was the longest one she'd ever had. The air was crisp and cold in the early morning sun as she and Bobby climbed down from the wagon and made their way toward the campfire where the same women from last night were bustling back and forth.

"Good morning, Kimberly. I didn't want to wake you. How are you feeling?"

Kim stared at Adeline.

"Okay, I guess," she said softly.

Another woman handed her a mug of hot steaming coffee and a slice of hard bread. Just then, there was the sound of a shout and horses. Five men on horseback, the carcasses of small game animals tied to their saddles, rode into camp. Kim's eyes opened wide as she realized that one of them was Marc, still dressed in the brown muslin shirt and heavier dark brown pants he'd had on last night when this dream or whatever it was began. Underneath his wide-brimmed leather hat, familiar brown eyes stared out at Kim. Was this really the same college student she knew and cared for? His face was thin, his hair was long and dirty, and he had a full beard and mustache.

One of the older men patted Marc on the shoulder as he dismounted.

"You might better lie down a spell after that fainting. I don't think you've quite recovered."

Kim stood at the edge of the group and spoke softly to Marc as he approached.

Another of the men passed by.

"You take good care of that man of yours," he said to Kim. "He fainted dead away on us for almost five minutes."

Marc's eyes met Kim's.

"Has it merged yet for you?" he whispered.

"Merged?"

"Look at that man over by the campfire – the one who just spoke to us."

"Okay."

"What's his name?"

"Benjamin Fuller, our leader."

"How did you know that?"

"I don't know," Kim whispered.

Suddenly her mind was filled with vivid images. An older couple hugging her. The woman was crying. Kim felt her heart ache. That had been her mother. They were telling her good-bye and they didn't believe they would ever see her again. But what about her real mother? Her mother and father and her brother, Brandon, in Salem, Oregon? She'd had dinner with them just last night... hadn't she? October 22, 1998. Kim shook her head, trying to clear it.

"It's happening to you, too, isn't it?" Marc said.

"Where are we?" Kim asked.

"It'll all start coming to you if you pay attention to what's in your mind, Kim."

He reached out and touched her gently on the arm.

"We're on the Oregon Trail."

"But why?"

"It's 1845, Kim."

Kim stood absolutely still, her mouth open.

"We're behind another wagon train that left two weeks before us. One that had 500 head of cattle going out to set up farms in Oregon. I gather ours was sort of an after thought – a lot of people who decided in a hurry that they wanted to get to Oregon and they wanted to get there this year."

"Why is everyone so thin and dirty and…?" Kim plucked the folds of her own soiled skirt.

"Look at your feet," Marc told her.

Kim stared at her dirt-covered boots and shifted from one aching foot to another.

"You've walked a good part of the way."

"From Missouri?" Kim gasped and then gasped even harder as memories began to flood her brain.

"We lost a week when Bobby's parents died in a river accident and we had to repair several of the wagons. Basically, Kim, we're all starving to death, and no one is even sure we're going to make it."

He got off his thin horse who began nibbling eagerly at some sparse meadow grass. Kim rubbed the horse's neck.

"Poor Rosie; you're so hungry," and then realizing she'd just said the horse's name, Kim looked at Marc. "This is your horse, right?"

"Since I was twelve," he answered.

"Today is a rest day to help the oxen and the horse teams recover. Tomorrow, we move toward the mountains."

"Marc?"

Marc looked tenderly at Kim whose eyes were filled with tears.

"Does the world we used to live in count for anything? Did it really exist?" she asked.

"That's what I've been trying to figure out all morning. I'm wondering if this is a dream or if that was?"

Just then, Bobby came running up red-faced with excitement.

"They're under the wagon. Under the wagon!" he repeated.

"What's under the wagon?" Kim asked.

But instead of answering her, he grabbed Kim and Marc by the hands and led them to the back of the Burchart wagon where they'd slept all night.

"There," he said pointing importantly as Marc and Kim bent down to look behind the wheels.

"I don't believe this," Marc said.

Marc stood up, both of their 1998 survival backpacks from the club meeting in his arms. The canvas was a little scorched but otherwise they appeared to be intact. Kim opened hers and peered inside. Everything was there – granola bars, chocolate, two meter rig. Marc pulled his two meter transceiver from his and pushed the on button. It was no surprise to either of them when they were greeted by silence. He turned it off and stuffed it back in the pack.

"I think we need to hide these," he said as he watched Emil walking across the clearing toward them.

Kim felt too confused to know what to do, but she climbed inside the wagon and put the bags under some quilts in the corner.

"MARCUS!"

Benjamin Fuller was yelling to him.

"There's work to do," the leader yelled.

"I'd better go."

Kim watched Marc as he joined the older man and disappeared behind some wagons.

"Why did you hide the radio stuff?" Bobby asked. "Can't you call my mommie and daddy now?"

"I don't think it's quite that simple, Bobby. But maybe we'll figure out something, okay? For now, let's have the radios be our secret."

Bobby nodded solemnly and clung to Kim's hand as she led him back to the campfire where the women were busy with morning chores.

"I'm sorry, Adeline," Kim said to the kind-faced woman as she helped her put away what was left of the meager foodstuffs.

With a start, Kim realized that she knew everyone's name in the group and most of their histories. Adeline Burchart, who was handling the reins of the team hitched to their wagon with authority, was married to Emil. It was their wagon that she and Bobby were riding in. A childless couple in their fifties, the Burcharts were emigrating to Oregon to be near a brother and his family who had emigrated the year before.

And it was Adeline who had offered to "chaperone" Kim on the trip to Oregon until she was married to... Kim definitely felt her heart skip more than one beat... Marc.

Suddenly, the scene in her parents' parlor flashed through her mind.

"I don't see why you young folks don't get married now," her mother had said.

"Marcus wants to wait until we get to Oregon. He wants our life together to begin in a home he's going to build."

"Well I don't think it's proper to be traveling together like that."

"Mother, I'm going to be with the Burcharts. You are so old-fashioned."

Kim smiled as she remembered that remark and for a second wondered if it was her 1840's mother or her 1990's mother who had said it. Neither mother need have worried because Adeline was taking her role as chaperone seriously. If Kim and Marc disappeared from her view for more than a few seconds, she was out scouting for them, often shouting, "Kimberly... Marcus" in a shrill voice that made them come running, red-faced with embarrassment.

She and Marc had known each other from childhood. It seemed as if they had always been friends in the little one room school in Independence, Missouri where she had grown up. It was the smallness of that school room that had brought them close together. The teacher, Miss Barnes, had been perplexed as to why these two children, both from farm families, had seemed so frustrated with the curriculum she offered.Usually, her problem was getting students to learn the basics: reading, writing, and arithmetic. But Kim and Marc were different. They seemed to inhale knowledge. When they studied Columbus, Marc wanted to know the exact dimensions of the sailing ships and begged for better explanations of the navigation tools they used.

When Miss Barnes tried, without success, to have her class read Julius Caesar, Kim memorized long sections of the text. She pleaded with Miss Barnes until she was able to find a complete works of William Shakespeare for her. Kim stayed after school each day to sweep the floors and wash the blackboards to pay for the thick book.

Other students soon learned not to bother to ask Kim and Marc to join in lunchtime games of hide and seek or ball under the shady trees that flanked their play area. The two of them could always be found sitting on a bench together discussing philosophy or religion or their favorite... science. It was Marc who climbed a tree to drop an apple and a feather from a limb, and it was Kim who stood at the bottom timing their fall. It was Marc who brought in a dead raccoon he found by the river and Kim who made the first incision into its belly to look at the intestines.

My dad's butchering a hog, Saturday," a boy taunted. "Want to come see it?"

"I know what the inside of a hog looks like," Marc said quietly. "I just never had seen inside a raccoon."

Kim, busy laying the various parts of the animal out on a board, ignored the boy, and Marc joined her in making sketches of the animal's internal structures.

The two were sixteen before they became interested in electricity. Marc had a book titled "Electricity, a Force in the Universe," that his uncle, a printer in Boston, had sent to him. The two read it from cover to cover and Marc even managed to make a battery similar to the one invented by Volta, but beyond that they hadn't done much. Then one day, that same uncle sent him a newspaper clipping about two men named Samuel F.B. Morse and Alfred Vail who were trying to prove to the world that messages could be sent through wire by electricity.

"It makes sense," Marc told Kim at lunch. "No matter how long a wire is, electricity will flow through it instantly. If there's an electro-magnet like Ampere's at the other end, electricity sent through the wire around the electro-magnet will make the magnet pick up iron. Then if you stop the electrical current, the iron will drop."

"And?" Kim questioned.

"Morse has developed a code – a pattern of sending and stopping the current that will mean words," Marc said.

"How far will the signals go?" Kim asked, smiling with excitement.

"As far as the wires. The experiment that I read about in the paper said a message was sent three miles."

"Three miles!" Kim exclaimed.

"And there's another man named Henry who's invented a relay.

"What's a relay?"

Marc thought a minute before answering. He loved explaining things to people but he knew that Kim got angry if she thought he was simplifying things too much. This girl had a brain every bit as quick as his, so he chose his words carefully.

"Let's say you have a stagecoach line. You want to get a message somewhere fast – say one hundred miles away. One team of horses can't run fast that far so every few miles you have a fresh set waiting."

"Yes," Kim encouraged him to go on.

"At say ten miles, the electric current is getting weak, sort of like the tired horses. But the current is still strong enough to work a little switch and put a fresh battery on the line. So every few miles, there are fresh batteries just as the stage has fresh horses."

"How long would it take to receive the message at the other end?" Kim asked.

"Oh, it would go instantly."

"My goodness," Kim said.

"But that's not the end of the story,' Marc said. "Morse believes that wires can be laid across the ocean and that someday, messages will be sent around the world."

At that, Kim had gazed into Marc's eyes with disbelief, but when she saw that he believed what he was saying, her disbelief turned to wonder.

"Do you know what Morse's first message was?"

"What?" Kim asked.

"What hath God wrought?"

Chapter 4

"What Hath God Wrought?"

Kim climbed into the wagon and pushed through food stuff barrels, mostly empty now, to a wooden trunk that was squeezed in against the edge of the wagon. She thought she knew what was in it, but she wanted to be sure. Kneeling on the wooden floor, she lifted the lid and gently pulled tissue paper from the white silk garment underneath.

Kim's eyes filled with tears as she held the delicate wedding gown in her hands. *So it was true. She was going to Oregon to marry Marc and here was the dress her mother and aunt had worked on so lovingly.* Kim traced her finger across the row of pearls along the neckline and then carefully put the dress back in the trunk. With a sigh, she closed the lid and stood up.

Kim's thoughts swirled as she helped Adeline sweep the trail dust out of the wagon. Caught between the real world she'd left in 1998 and the remembered one of her past in Missouri, she felt pulled and tugged emotionally to the point of exhaustion. She tried to focus on the chores at hand and mentally counted the hours until evening would come when she might have a chance to talk to Marc in greater depth.

Around the clearing on "their day of rest," women went through the familiar daily routine of re-organizing what was left of their precious possessions. With every meal, the barrels in the wagons became lighter and the need to reach Oregon more urgent. From looking at their faces though, it would be hard to tell their fears. All of them worked steadily with a calm serenity. Kim thought about each person in the group, everyone of them different, but all brought together in a common quest – Oregon.

There were the Simmons: William, Mary, and three year old Anthony. Their baby girl had been stillborn near Fort Laramie. Mary, pale and grim-faced, had clung to her husband and son at the infant's small funeral. The wagon train rested a half day and then Adeline and Kim made an extra soft bed of quilts for the woman to lie on inside the wagon.

The baby had not been the only loss. Of an original party of thirty-seven, thirty-one remained. Bobby's parents had drowned in a Wyoming river when their wagon overturned and they were swept away. Somehow, the currents that carried them down river had driven the little boy to shore where others pulled him out. It took two hours before the men, searching on horseback, found his dead parents floating in the river, their possessions scattered along the river banks. The team of oxen stood in the mud, remnants of the wagon still attached to their harness. The men salvaged what they could and brought the oxen back to the group. Bobby's parents were buried with the smashed tops of wooden dressers serving as coffins.

Fifty-four year old Adeline, who had never been able to have children of her own, became an instant mother to anyone in need. Bobby was placed in their wagon, where, under the ministrations of Kim and Adeline and Emil, he began to heal.

Joseph Bell, 59, had died of consumption. Henrietta Maisley, who at the age of 84, had insisted she didn't want to leave Missouri, had been forced along by her son, John, who said there was no one to care for her in Independence. He pleaded with her, promising a beautiful log cabin in Oregon with a bedroom all her own. In the end, she agreed to go, but not before she had the local coffin maker construct a box engraved with her initials. Henrietta didn't wake up one morning, and she was buried in her personalized coffin in a clearing in Southwest Nebraska.

One man, Alexander Josten, simply disappeared. He said he was going out hunting one day and he didn't come back. They never found his body and they never found his horse. There was lots of conjecture about whether he had been taken by Indians, had fallen off a cliff, or had simply run off on his own. The latter seemed unthinkable as perils were everywhere and the group clung together not only for companionship, but for safety.

All of this was present in Kim's mind as she tried to come to terms with the reality of her present combined with the future that she had been so happy in just 24 hours ago. And somehow mingled with the very real memories of yesterday was the knowledge of the home she'd left in Missouri. She'd just been offered a job as teacher at the one room school where she and Marc had gone. Miss Barnes, at the ripe old age of 42, had finally gotten married and was planning on moving to Kansas City with her husband, a horse trader.

Kim thought her life was set. She would teach school and Marc would work at carpenter jobs until the two of them could save enough money to start his dream – a lumber mill. Then he heard about Oregon where supposedly the trees grew so thick you couldn't see through them. Tales of abundant water, rich soil that grew unbelievable crops, and land just there for the settling.

"With all the emigrants going to Oregon, there'll be a great need for teachers," Marc told her. "I'll build you a school house; I'll build us a home; I'll build us a future."

So insistent on proving to her that their life would be perfect in the far distant land of Oregon, Marc said he would not marry her until they were there – until she saw for herself that he kept his promises.

"And if it doesn't work out exactly as you said, what then?" she asked him. "Will you not marry me?"

"I'll send you back to Independence and you can marry Jesse White. He's had his eye on you for a long time."

Kim laughed. Jesse, the owner of the livery stable, was middle-aged, overweight, and he smoked big black cigars that surrounded him with noxious blue smoke continually.

"You will not," Kim told him. "When we get to Oregon, you will marry me no matter what. Say you will or I won't go."

"I will," Marc said softly.

So here they were, tired, footsore, hungry, and mourning the loss of their traveling companions. Yet, at night, the talk around the campfire was not about what they had left behind, but about what lay ahead. The closer they got to their final destination of the Willamette Valley, the more intense the fervor of the group grew.

The house on Main Street that Kim had envisioned with its perfect rose garden and white picket fence was never going to happen. There would be no dinners in the dining room with her parents and grandparents admiring the perfect meal she had cooked or the shine of the china on the beautifully-set table. Instead, she was on her way to the unknown, a set of crockery, embroidered linens, and her wedding dress as her dowry.

Her parents had talked about sending her grandmother's china with her, but the wagon master, Mr. Fuller, said it would very likely break on the jouncy trail and the numerous lowerings down steep cliffs. Besides, they needed every square inch for supplies. The wedding dress was only allowed to be brought when Kim showed how the dress could rest on top of bags of dried beans in the trunk. Now the beans were gone, and the dress had the cedar chest to itself.

Kim felt a lump in her throat at the thought of getting married without her parents there. *But which parents?* The faces of her mother and father in Missouri blurred with those of her parents in Salem until they seemed like the same people. Kim shook her head to clear it.

"What's the matter, Kimberly?" Adeline asked. "You've been acting strangely all day. Are you still feeling unwell?"

"Just thinking."

"It doesn't do any good to ponder things too closely. Just think about the future. That's what your life is now."

Kim tried to smile at the advice but there was something in Adeline's voice that made her feel a deep chill inside. It was obvious that the woman didn't really believe in the future. Kim tried to shake off the fear overwhelming her but it was very real.

"Adeline?"

"Yes?"

"You don't think we're going to reach Oregon, do you?"

The woman looked at Kim with surprise. It was an unwritten law that they never voiced their fears. Fears given words could become panic. Better to keep them to yourself. She looked away.

"Adeline?"

"What child?"

"I think we will, but we have to get there quickly."

At that, Adeline laughed.

"And how do you think we will get there quickly, Kimberly? The worst part of the journey is still to be done. And look around you. We have no food. The oxen and horses are barely alive. And we have no time. We're going to have to wait every step of the way now while the men go ahead and find the best places to cross rivers and to pasture the animals. And then we have to wait for them to come back and tell us. If we take even one wrong turn, we're all dead..." She paused. "And maybe even if we don't," she added quietly.

In mid-afternoon, there was a shout from the perimeter and everyone rushed to see. Charles Harley, a single man in the group, was approaching on foot, leading a steer that barely looked alive.

"Look what I found!" he yelled. "It must have strayed from the Olson train ahead of us."

The trail in the last few weeks had been littered with the carcasses of dead animals. This was the first live one they'd seen. There was no need to discuss what to do. Kim watched as several of the men, including Marc, led the animal to the rear of the wagons, killed it, and butchered it on the spot.

"Well don't just stand there, Kimberly," Adeline said. "Help me gather some wood."

Kim searched for branches from the young cottonwoods that grew along the stream. It was the first real firewood they'd had in weeks. Soon, the women had the fire blazing, and Kim felt her stomach clench in hunger as the aroma of roasting beef filled the air. The delicious smell seemed to infuse new energy into the group. Women began boiling water to wash clothing, a sure sign of their optimism.

Kim slipped into another dress, not quite as soiled as the one she was wearing, and gathered up an armful of underthings. Just as she was climbing out of the wagon, a lump in the hem of the dress she'd just taken off caught her eye. Thinking that she'd caught some pebbles in the fold of material, Kim turned the edge of the dress to see if she could shake them out. Two dozen white pills fell into her hand. Kim gazed at them in amazement and then raised her hand to sniff them. They had the unmistakable moldy smell of Penicillin.

What on earth? Were these the pills Dr. Harrison prescribed for her? They certainly looked like them. It was then that Kim realized that her sore throat from 150 years in the future was gone, and she found herself shaking her head in bewilderment. *Hey folks, she would say at a medical convention. I've found the perfect cure for Strep throat. All you need is a Spark Gap transmitter and...*

Kim collected the pills in her palm and climbed back in the wagon where she hid them in a small bag behind some barrels in the corner. Outside, scrubbing her clothing by the stream, she couldn't stop thinking about what she had just found. Her mind had come from the future or from the present to the past. She was too confused to decide what was what. And somehow she was in another girl's body – one that looked exactly like her. And a few things had come along with her. *Why?* she thought as she scrubbed and scrubbed her clothes and then rinsed them in the clear, running water of the creek. *Why? Why? Why?*

She looked over at Bobby as he walked over to play with Jasper, an eight year old boy, the youngest son of the Harrington family. The two squatted in the dirt and fashioned a fort out of sticks and leaves. Kim noticed that ever since midday, Bobby seemed to be less and less concerned about his whereabouts and how he got here. In fact, it was hard to tell watching him now that he had ever lived in any other time period. *Was he forgetting? Was that what would happen to her too? Another day and the Kim of the future would cease to exist?* Kim clenched her fists and vowed that she would retain her memories – all of them.

At dusk, while the wet laundry fluttered in the breeze, everyone gathered around and ate slabs of the meat, the juices running down their hands. What was left was salted and stored in empty barrels in the wagons. Usually their main meal was at noon, but the meat they were eating hadn't made its appearance until later.

The people were so hungry that there was little conversation during the meal but when their appetites were sated, the men began to talk. Fueled by the fresh beef, their hopes rose once again and the stories began to fly.

"I've heard the fish are so thick in the streams, they jump right out into your hands."

"The soil grows corn sweeter and juicier than any we've ever seen."

"More deer and elk than you can shake a stick at."

As the people talked, Kim moved to the edge of the group. Marc saw her get up and soon joined her. They walked around behind the wagons, away from view. Marc gathered her in his arms and held her close. Neither spoke for several moments.

"We don't even drive through the mountains in November without four wheel drive or carrying chains," Kim said. "These people are never going to make it."

"They will if they don't waste any time," Marc said. "Once they start moving, they've got to keep going. There can't be time lost to scouting."

"Oh sure, and if they just forge ahead and get to some impassable place, what are they going to do then?" Kim asked.

"That's not going to happen," Marc said quietly. "I'm going to go ahead and search it out and radio the information back to you."

"Radio?"

"On our two meter rigs, Kim. We ought to be able to use simplex for five or so miles."

Kim laughed.

"First of all, these people would never believe you and if you demonstrated the radios, do you know what'd they think?"

"What?"

"Well burning witches at the stake comes to mind. Did people in the 1840's believe in little green men from Mars? That's another possibility," Kim said. "If we're stuck here, I don't want to be lynched or stoned or something."

"You really think they'd do that?" Marc asked.

"I don't know but I'm sure they wouldn't understand. And people tend not to like what they don't understand."

"Okay," Marc said slowly. "Then we'll do it another way. Apparently, I'm the boy scientist and you're my able assistant, from what I can remember. I've got a news article in my trunk about Morse and it looks like I've been trying to re-create his work with home-brew batteries and telegraph keys. These people all know about that. In fact, they laugh about it because so far my experiment hasn't worked at all. I'm not sure what's wrong with the batteries but they're not sending any current through the wire."

"What are you suggesting, Marc?"

"We've got to trick them."

"How?"

"Disguise our equipment to look like the stuff I'm working on."

Adeline's Diary

October 22, 1845

Dear Diary:

Yesterday was another day without seeing a flower alongside the road. How I miss the sweet fragrance of the roses back home. The beautiful red rose Emil dug up for me and put in the bucket is still alive. He says once we get to Oregon, he will plant it right by the front door of our new house.

We were disappointed that the lone pine we'd heard about at this campground had been cut down by some inconsiderate soul. Not a tree near, but we and the animals are grateful to be camped next to the Powder River.

The strangest thing happened today. Kimberly has always been the first one to wake in the morning. In fact, she is often reading those books of hers before the sun is fully up. This morning, she and young Robert just slept and slept. They looked so tired I didn't have the heart to wake them and since we weren't traveling today, I let them sleep.

Then when they finally did wake up, they were both of them talking so strange, it made me wonder. Kimberly even asked for sugar and milk for her cereal. How could she ever forget the sight of poor Bessie drowned in the river?

Sometimes, I wish she had married Marcus before we left on this journey. I promised her parents I would look after her and that I will, but if she gets strange in the head, I don't know what I will do. Let's hope it's just a passing spell.

We've spent the day resting which the Good Lord knows we surely need. I think the days ahead will be harder than any of us has ever imagined. But God has brought us this far and I trust He will provide. Today, when we were all wondering how to make six rabbits feed us all, a cow from the Olsons appeared. Trust in the Lord. It's hard when you're hungry, but we must.

October 22, 1845

Oh one more thing, Dear Diary. Here I've been carrying on and talking about folks and I've never written all their names down. I think I'll do so now so there'll be a record of all us. There were 37 of us and 10 wagons when we left Independence. Now there are just 31 and 8 wagons. Of course, leading us are the Fullers. That's Benjamin and his dear wife May Belle. Their children are all grown. One daughter and her husband are already in Oregon. The other daughter and son and their families live in Kansas.

Behind them is the Simmons' wagon. That's William and Mary and little Anthony. They are a sweet, hopeful

32

family, and William has about got their wagon filled to over-flowing with crop seed and farm tools. He says he's going to grow so much in Oregon that he alone could feed the whole territory.

Next in line are the Harringtons — Nigel, Marissa, and their three children: John, Melanie, and Jasper. Nigel is a lawyer and he thinks with all the people flooding to Oregon, he'll have a good business.

Frances and James Dearborn are the oldest couple in the group, next to us that is, and I'm not telling how old I am. Emil is 59.

Alexander and Carolyn Malby are intelligent people. I enjoy listening to them talk. Alexander was a carpenter back in Independence and he and Marcus have plans to go into business together. Jack and Hannah Worth are new-lyweds and they're expecting a baby.

Then there's the Hodges: Grayson, Susan, and little Andrew. Grayson hopes to open a general store when we get there.

That's all of the families. Kimberly is riding with us. The single men: Marcus, Charles Harley, Thomas Amalind, Robert Maisley, Mitchell Copeland, and Richard Faley have their belongings in a wagon together. Most of them don't own much. They're bringing a little money and a lot of hope.

Chapter 5

"Keep Your Powder Dry"

Thomas Amalind, better known for his drinking binges than his wit, repeated that expression over and over as they moved the wagon train along the Powder River the next day. No one laughed but Thomas was his own best audience. He required no encouragement.

Keeping anything dry, let alone gun powder, was difficult, in some of the river crossings. The men hunted carefully for good fording places – places where previous wagon trains had put logs on the bottom for the wheels to travel across. Where there were trees to chop down, they made their own fords. Sometimes, they spent hours raising the levels of the wagons in an attempt to keep things dry, but they weren't always successful. About the only positive aspect in crossing a river or stream, oftentimes over and over again in search of a better trail, was that it cooled the aching feet of the walkers... and of course, it was that much closer to their final goal.

Today, Kim trudged along reflecting on all that had happened in the last 24 hours. She still hadn't completely "merged" as Marc called it. Salem, Oregon seemed a lot more real to her than here; however, the exhaustion she felt was convincing. And hour by hour, her traveling companions and their idiosyncrasies were emerging from fuzziness into reality.

For instance, Adeline liked things "just so." Kim bet that she was the type of housekeeper who never changed the position of a single piece of furniture. No wonder her parents had assigned her the role of chaperoning Kim. Adeline had a strict set of rules and she expected everyone to abide by them.

Last night before she'd gone to bed, Adeline had surprised Kim by handing her a small leather-bound book.

"Aren't you going to write in your diary?"she asked.

With a start, Kim opened the book and read the previous entries. Many of the same thoughts that had flooded through her mind when the past and future merged were recorded here. And the handwriting even looked like hers!

Oh how I long to be in our home with my beloved Marcus, she'd written the week before. *Sometimes during the day when I feel so weary that I don't believe I can take another step, I simply close my eyes and imagine how it will be. If anything, we have less time to talk to each other on this journey than we did at home. The men expect him to be with them all the time. They're always fixing wagons, riding ahead to check on the trail, or hunting for food. Will this journey never be over? Will we never have time just to sit and share our ideas?*

Kim skimmed through the pages and then handed the book back to Adeline who was busy recording her own thoughts for the day.

"I'm just too tired to write tonight," Kim said as she lay down and pulled the covers up over her shoulders.

That apparently hadn't set well with Adeline because the first thing she'd done this morning when Kim woke up was to hand her the diary.

"You write your thoughts from last night and I'll go help with breakfast,"Adeline commanded, climbing out of the wagon.

Why would Adeline care whether she wrote in her diary or not? Kim wondered. And then a suspicion came to her that she realized the Kim of the 1800's had been harboring for a long time. Adeline was probably sneaking peeks into the diary. Perhaps Kim's chronicles of her romantic thoughts about Marc were entertainment for the old woman.

Kim penned a few lines, being careful not to make any reference to what had really happened to her the day before. She replaced the book on a small ledge high above the barrels where it was unlikely to get wet. There were six other books on the shelf: the Bible, Adeline's diary, Emil's record of family history and finances, and three of Kim's science books. Kim pushed her diary in so that it was slightly out of line with the others.

Sure enough, when Kim came back to the wagon after eating their meager breakfast, the book was in line with all the others. Since the wagons hadn't begun to move yet, it was unlikely that anything other than a human hand had moved it. Of course, it was always possible that Adeline had just lined them up to be tidy, but Kim doubted it. She made a mental note to herself to be careful of what she wrote.

She wondered what it was that Marc planned to make, but she didn't see him until the noonday meal when he and two other men came back to report to the others about the trail ahead. Kim noted that Benjamin Fuller had stayed behind with the women instead of riding ahead as he usually did. He'd been coughing for the last week and it looked as if he felt worse today. They'd already buried one man from pneumonia along the trail. Illness was a constant worry for all of them. In their worn-down state, any of them could be vulnerable.

Now, Benjamin sat with the others around the campfire while Alexander Malby told the group what lay ahead.

"There's a good camp site ahead six miles out. We can get there easily before dark and then tomorrow, we should reach the Grande Ronde Valley."

Alexander looked at Marc for his confirmation as he spoke.

"We took a look at the trail down. It's a steep one all right, but we can make it."

Marc nodded in agreement. They looked at Benjamin Fuller, but he was having a coughing spell. His wife patted him on the back.

"Maybe we should rest another day so Ben can get back on his feet," suggested William Simmons.

"No, no," came the answer from many of the group. Alexander pointed at the sky filled with wispy gray clouds that seemed to be moving with unusual speed.

"We should move on," Benjamin said, wiping his mouth with a handkerchief. "Winter's not going to wait forever."

They packed their eating utensils, yoked the oxen, and pulled out of the resting place. The rest of the afternoon went smoothly. Just before they reached their evening resting place, two eastbound horsemen bearing sacks of flour and a small amount of sugar purchased in the Dalles, came upon them. Their names were Jed and Herman Willits, twin brothers, and they were on their way back home to fetch their families from Missouri.

The wagon train was eager to purchase flour and sugar from them and invited the men to have supper and share their stories. After the wagons were drawn into place, and the animals turned out to graze, the people sat around and listened to Jed and Herman talk while supper cooked.

Yes, they had come through the Blue Mountains and yes the trail was difficult, but not so bad without wagons. There was a little snow on the ground near the summit but nothing serious yet. And yes, Oregon was everything they'd heard. They had been there for six months and now they were hoping to make good time getting back to their families. Their plan was to winter in Missouri and then head west again in spring. The emigrants hung on every word.

While the group was absorbed in the talk, Kim and Marc moved away quietly, one at a time so as not to attract attention. They met behind Adeline and Emil's wagon.

"Can you find two wooden boxes about this big?" Marc asked Kim gesturing with his hands.

"How about the ones I keep my beads in?"

"They ought to do."

Peeking around the corner at the group swapping tales of hope around the fire, Kim crept into the wagon where she slept. Charles Harley had gotten out his violin now and his clear melodies sent an ache of nostalgia through Kim. It had been weeks since he'd played. All of them had been too exhausted at night to do little more than collapse into sleep.

Tonight was different.. They had eaten; they had renewed hope. These were songs of celebration… or of farewell, Kim thought as she rummaged through the box that held her belongings.

She found the wooden boxes wrapped in a quilt at the bottom of a crate. Each of them was about a foot long, eight inches wide, and six inches high. They had once held her grandfather's cigars, and she could still smell their pungent aroma as she opened the lids. Inside one was a string of pearls from her grandmother and in the other, several necklaces of glass beads she had collected over the years. All of the women had brought extra strands of glass beads to trade to the Indians for goods. Kim was saving these to use as barter in Oregon. She wrapped the remaining necklaces in one of the linen pillowcases her grandmother had made and placed the small bundle in the bottom of her wedding dress trunk. With a sigh, she smoothed the folds of the wedding dress and closed the lid.

"Perfect," Marc said when she handed the boxes and his backpack to him.

"How are you going to work on it without them seeing what you're doing?"

"After everyone is asleep, I guess. I'll have to go off where no one can see me," Marc said. "I've got a flashlight."

The sound of the group singing filled the air.

"Oh God, our help in ages past,
  Our hope for years to come,
  Our shelter from the stormy blast,
  And our eternal home."

The lyrics echoed in Kim's and Marc's ears as they crept away from the group. A hundred yards from the edge of the camp, they hid the pack in some scrub brush. Kim turned to question Marc.

"So when you demonstrate this marvelous invention, is it going to be with a wire or without?"

"I think we'll try it with a wire first," Marc said, "and then if they seem to believe that, you and I will pretend to experiment without the wire. We'll be as surprised as they are when it works."

"Indeed we will," Kim said.

For a minute she had slipped back into the easy, humorous banter that characterized the relationship between the two of them, but the aching fatigue in her body was an all too real reminder of where they were. Arm in arm, they walked slowly back toward the group whose voices seemed to be lifted heavenward by the flickering flames at their center.

"Time, like an ever-rolling stream,
Bears all its own away;
They fly, forgotten as a dream
Dies at the opening day."

Kim reached out and stroked Marc's gaunt cheek. He put his arms around her and held her close as the hymn came to its triumphant end.

"O God, our help in ages past,
Our hope for years to come,
Be thou our guide while life shall last,
And our eternal home."

Kim laid her face against the rough fabric of Marc's shirt. She didn't realize she was crying until he reached down and wiped her tears with his hand.

"It's going to be okay," he whispered to her.

"We'll never get back," she said.

"If we don't, we'll just be here together. Together in Oregon. Oregon Territory," he added.

He lifted her face with his hands and smiled at her.

"I've been listening to the men talk, and you know that Willamette Valley sounds pretty neat."

He chuckled.

"I wanted to tell them about I-5, the shopping malls, McDonald's, the Indian casinos, the Rose Garden..."

"Do you think the Blazers will win this year?" Kim laughed.

"Which year?"

She pressed her face against his chest.

"We didn't realize how easy our life was then," she said quietly. "I'd take a calculus midterm every day over this."

Their time together was interrupted by the piercing call of Adeline.

"Kimberly, come help me!"

Kim ran to the campfire. The women were scurrying in various directions.

"Hannah's baby's coming," Adeline told her.

A wave of fear swept Kim. Hannah was petite, her hips barely wider than those of a young boy's. Kim knew everyone was hoping that her baby would be late and that they'd somehow get over the mountains to the settlements beyond where there would be a doctor to help.

Kim had seen lots of baby calves and horses born, but she'd never witnessed a human birth. The 1990's part of her brain told her that surely, Jack, Hannah's husband, would be by her side to help her every step of the way. The 1840's part countered that this was woman's work, and she, as Hannah's closest friend in the group, would be expected to be on hand. Kim ran to Hannah and Jack's wagon.

Adeline Burchart and Frances Dearborn were positioning Hannah on a pile of quilts and trying to soothe her. Just from watching dramas about childbirth on television, Kim knew that Hannah wasn't very far along, but already she was wild-eyed with fear. Kim crawled up near her and took her hand.

"You're okay, Hannah. I'm right here," she reassured her.

Hannah gasped and clutched at her abdomen.

"Is another one starting?" Kim asked.

40

"Yessss," Hannah moaned.

"Listen Hannah, look at me."

Hannah tossed her head around, looking everywhere but at Kim.

"Look at me," Kim insisted.

Hannah's frightened eyes turned to Kim.

"Keep your eyes on mine and breathe in and out slowly... like this," Kim demonstrated taking long, slow breaths.

Adeline and Frances watched curiously as gradually Kim calmed Hannah and got her into a measured breathing exercise to take her mind off her pain. Had they known that Kim's knowledge was coming from a scene she'd once seen on Days of Our Lives, they would have been even more bewildered. But whatever it was Kim was doing to Hannah, hypnotism or just the power of friendship, Hannah was visibly relaxing, and the women knew that was good.

When Hannah seemed more in control, Kim took time to look around her. The quilts she was lying on were visibly soiled from the trail dust and nights of their dirty bodies sleeping in them.

Kim looked at the women and searched her brain. In her biology classes, they had touched on the great pioneers in science. Lister, Pasteur, Jenner. For the life of her, she couldn't remember the dates. The only thing that came to mind was an article written by Oliver Wendell Holmes about the dangers of childbirth fever and his theory that it was passed from patient to patient by midwives and doctors. Kim closed her eyes and tried to see the date at the top of the biology text. *1824?* That seemed about right. So people were at least talking about germs in the 1840's. But from what she could see around her, it didn't look like anyone in this group was too concerned.

"Just a minute," Kim said.

She gave Hannah's hand a quick squeeze and crawled to the opening of the wagon. She ran across the clearing and climbed into her wagon. Bobby was fast asleep in the quilts, his face still smeared with the beef juice. Quietly, Kim knelt by the box of her linens and pulled out a large tablecloth and a stack of pillowcases. They weren't sterile by any means, but they were a far sight cleaner than what the women were planning to use.

She ran back to Hannah's wagon.

"Oh Kimberly, those are your wedding linens. Don't let them get soiled."

"That's just the point," Kim said. "It's better to have them get dirty than Hannah."

She looked around at the women: Adeline, Frances, and now joined by a third one - Carolyn Malby, a grandmother who considered herself the expert on the "birthing process."

"There's a tiny sliver of lye soap left by the wash basin. I don't want anyone touching Hannah without washing her hands with it first," Kim told them in a commanding tone.

"Well," said Carolyn indignantly. "Aren't you the little miss know it all?"

Adeline's Diary

October 23, 1845

Dear Diary:

I believe it is already the 24th, but I am still awake and as I always pen a few lines before sleep, I see no reason not to do so tonight. The fire is blazing, giving warmth for poor Jack as he waits for his young wife, Hannah, to give birth. I am sitting here also, but he is absorbed in his thoughts as I am in mine.

Hannah's cries must be keeping everyone awake although they have lessened some since Kimberly starting having her breathe strangely. It is really the oddest thing I have seen. Here, Frances and I were taking care of her the way we have done countless times and Kimberly appeared with some strange notion about Hannah breathing a certain way, panting like a dog really, and staring at her face. If you ask me, she's gone and hypnotized the poor girl, but I guess if it lessens her pain, there's no harm done. Kimberly has unusual ideas but perhaps that comes from all those books she's always reading.

It's going to be a long night for sure. In my prayers tonight will be Hannah and her unborn baby and also Benjamin Fuller. He's looking very unwell.

Tomorrow, we are supposed to get to the Grand Ronde Valley, but we will have to wait and see what morning brings.

Chapter 6

A New Voice

As the wagon train members tried to sleep, Hannah labored on, aided by Kim with an occasional visit from Frances, Adeline, and Carolyn. The older women's suggestions fell on deaf ears as Hannah and Kim seemed to have melded together in a common effort.

At one point, Kim told Frances to get Hannah's husband.

"Whatever on earth for?" Frances asked.

"Just go fetch him," Kim said.

A pale-faced Jack Worth entered the wagon a few minutes later. Kim wiped the sweat from Hannah's face and spoke to Jack.

"Come on up here; you can help."

Jack seemed reluctant but when Hannah reached out her hand toward him, he took it unhesitatingly and crawled up beside her.

Watching from the wagon opening, Frances and Carolyn shook their heads. This was not the way births were handled. Hannah began to moan again and Kim took her hand.

"Look at me, Hannah, and breathe. In and out slowly. In and out. That's good."

Jack, holding Hannah's other hand, took his cue from Kim and talked to his wife.

"Come on Hannah. We're going to have a beautiful baby. I'm here. It's okay."

****

A quarter of a mile from the wagon train, far enough to make sure that no one would find him, Marc sat on the ground, his invention pieces in front of him. If it weren't such serious business, he would have laughed at the crude telegraph keys in front of him, but he mentally gave himself credit for making them at all. He hunted through his bag of electrical parts and sat back on his heels to think about what he was going to do. Could he wire a switch that was triggered by the telegraph key that would then turn on his hidden transmitter?

"I don't have time for that," he said aloud. "If we're going to fool them, might as well make it big time."

He took a nail and gouged a hole through the wooden box so that the nail would barely slide through. Then he lined up his two meter transceiver (transmitter/receiver combination) in the box so that the on/off button was directly under the nail. He glued some blocks in place to hold it securely and then after setting the frequency on 146.52 simplex, he turned it off and closed it inside the box.

He pushed the nail in and heard the hiss of the transmitter turning on. He pushed it again and heard it click off. He fastened the box shut.

"The last thing I want is for someone to look inside," he said to the night. He attached the telegraph key to the box and attached a wire to the box. Now to do Kim's.

It was almost daybreak before he was done. As he walked back to camp he worried about a way to keep the batteries charged. If they were going to use these devices very much at all, it wouldn't be long until the two meter batteries went dead. Each of them had a spare, but what would happen when those were gone? He was eager to try out his solar charger but that would involve spreading the panels out in the sunshine for several hours at a time.

On top of one of the wagons. That was the logical place, Marc thought as he entered the camp. He'd have to invent some kind of a story to tell them about it. *Actually folks, I'm from 150 years ahead of you and this solar charger will power my two meter rig inside this box. What's a two meter rig? you ask. Well let's see. Maybe I should start with Marconi.*

Suddenly, Marc stopped. Was getting power from the sun such a far-fetched idea? Hadn't man realized the sun's magnificent potential since the beginning of time? Without sun, there would be no heat. Even these Midwesterners knew that a cool spring and summer meant delayed crop harvests.

****

Jack, sweating almost as hard as his wife, held onto her hand gamely. He had fallen into Kim's rhythmic breathing and the whole wagon was filled with the huffing and puffing of the trio.

After a particularly hard contraction, Kim wiped the sweat from Hannah's brow tenderly.

"Here comes another one," Hannah whispered.

"Breathe, breathe," Kim told her.

Out of the corner of her eye, Kim saw Caroline, Frances, and Adeline hovering in the background. Even as busy as she was, her brain registered the fact that if she didn't involve the women in the birth in some way that they were really going to be angry.

"I don't know anything about the birthing itself. You'll do that, won't you? Kim asked them humbly, and then added quietly, "Make sure you wash your hands first."

Frances mumbled something about it being big of her to admit that there was something in the world she didn't know. She and Adeline and Carolyn left the wagon and came back a few minutes later, their hands freshly scrubbed. Still holding Hannah's hands, Kim and Jack scooted back a few inches to allow them room.

****

"What on earth are you doing up there?" Emil Burchart asked Marc as he stretched the solar charging panels out on top of the their wagon.

"It's something Kim's uncle sent her from a science exposition he went to in Boston," Marc said. *Blame everything on Kim's fictitious uncle,* he thought. "It's all part of the ongoing experiments in electricity. People are trying to figure out the best way to keep batteries charged. These strips gather power from the sun and store it. Then we can connect our batteries to them."

"Well I'll be…" Emil said, scratching his beard. "Sounds like a lot of hocus pocus to me."

"You don't mind if I put them up here, do you? Guess I should have asked first," Marc said apologetically.

"Not if they don't interfere with the wagon, none, then I guess I don't care."

Marc watched Emil as he wandered off toward the other men, undoubtedly to tell the new crazy thing that Marc was up to.

****

Hannah's fingers clenched Kim's hand so hard, she wondered if they'd punctured her skin. With her eyes locked on Kim's, the laboring young woman took a huge breath and pushed it out with a yell that shook the wagon.

"It's coming; it's coming," Carolyn said. "Keep on pushing."

"Come on Hannah… PUSH!"

Hannah's entire body convulsed with the effort, but this time she did it, and as she fell limply back into Kim's arms, they were greeted by the welcome cry of her baby, soon cradled in Carolyn's arms. Frances reached over to wrap it in one of the pillowcases.

"It's a girl," Kim told her.

Jack, his face filled with emotion, bent down to kiss his wife. Frances wiped the baby clean and then handed the lustily-crying infant to her father. Jack's face filled with joy. He blinked back tears as he lowered the baby into his exhausted wife's arms.

"Kimberly," Hannah said weakly.

"What Hannah?" Kim asked.

"I'm going to name her Kimberly."

Kim sat back on her heels and basked in the glow of the new family. Even though Hannah was so tired she could barely keep her eyes open, she summoned enough strength to hold her new baby with Jack's supporting arm under hers. Little Kimberly, for all the difficulty she had arriving in the world, seemed hale and hearty. Her tiny arms and legs weren't as plump as babies Kim was used to seeing, but her lungs seemed as good as any and she was demonstrating them to their full advantage.

Outside at the campfire, the newborn's cries were a cause for celebration. Soon, Jack emerged from the wagon and the men clapped him on the back with congratulations. He seemed a little dazed from the emotional experience he had just witnessed and went from man to man describing with his hands just how small and perfect his daughter was.

Meanwhile, the women made flapjacks from the flour they'd bought from the travelers and everyone gathered around in a celebration breakfast. Kim ate one of the hot, delicious cakes and then crawled into the Burcharts' wagon to sleep.

She slept for two hours, but it only seemed like two minutes before Adeline shook her awake.

"Best to get up. We're going to move out soon," the woman told her.

Kim sat up and rubbed her eyes. Adeline hadn't had much sleep either but you'd never know it to look at her. She was fully dressed and obviously anxious to be underway.

"How's Hannah?" Kim asked.

"Pretty weak, but the little one... little Kimberly," Adeline almost smiled at Kim, "seems ready to get on the trail. Such a lusty pair of lungs. She's awfully thin, but aren't we all?" Adeline said, rubbing her own arms. "Let's hope Hannah's milk comes in good and rich."

Kim shook her head. Fat chance of that. She made a mental promise to herself to give part of her rations to Hannah.

"Before we leave, I understand Marcus is going to entertain everyone with some sort of magical message machine."

"Really?" Kim said innocently. "Well maybe I can help him."

"You two have your heads in the stars, that's what. Better to be thinking of practical things than all that trickery you do."

"I'll remember that," Kim said. "I'll go look in on Hannah."

Adeline started to reach for Kim's diary to hand it to her, but Kim shook her head.

"Not now. I'm so tired I can scarcely think. I'll write twice as much tonight," Kim told her.

She climbed down from the wagon. Everyone was making preparations to leave while being as quiet as they could out of concern for the resting Hannah. The campfire was almost out, but no one was sitting by it anyway. The women were busy inside the wagons, and the men were repairing the oxen yokes and mule harnesses. Kim approached Hannah's wagon and peeked in. Hannah was fast asleep on a pile of quilts. Jack sat protectively beside her, the baby wrapped in one of Kim's pillowcases between them. He held up a finger to caution Kim. He crawled over to the end of the wagon and climbed out.

"How is she?"

"I hope she's all right," Jack said. "She looks so tired. Not the lively Hannah I married last winter."

"She did a lot of hard work last night."

"I know, and I know how much you helped her, Kimberly. I'm grateful to you."

"Just take good care of her and that little baby," Kim said, patting his arm.

"Jack?" Hannah called out weakly from inside the wagon.

"I'm right here, dear," he said climbing back in.

Kim peeked in.

"How are you feeling?"

"I am fine," Hannah said, smiling at Kim, but her voice sounded anything but fine.

"I just thought of something," Kim said. "I'll be right back."

She turned and ran back to her wagon. She'd been so excited about finding their radio gear in the packs that she'd ignored all the rest of the items. At the bottom of each were some dried foodstuffs. *How could she explain that to the group?* Holding out food from the others was not acceptable behavior at all. More than one fist fight had broken out on wagon trains when someone was found to have a secret cache. Not only would the food stash be hard to explain; the grocery store labels would be impossible.

Kim crept into her wagon, grateful that neither Adeline nor Bobby was around. She dug down in the trunk underneath her wedding dress where she'd moved her backpack. There were two granola bars right on top. *Oatmeal with raisin. That ought to do the trick.* She unwrapped them, slipped them in her pocket, and crawled back out of the wagon.

There was no one by the fire so she threw the labels in, watching the green and yellow striped paper curl into the flames. Most of the dishes had been packed, but Adeline and Emil's box of crockery was still sitting by the cooking area. She found a bowl and crumbled the granola bars into it and added some boiling water. The sweet smell of the raisins and brown sugar was enough to make her feel faint, but Kim carried it quickly to Hannah's wagon.

"Where on earth did you get that?" Hannah asked her weakly as Kim spooned the hot cereal mixture into her mouth.

"Marc's uncle," Kim fibbed. "You know the one in Boston who sends him the newspaper clippings about scientific inventions. He mailed us a box that he said we weren't to open until we were almost to Oregon. I figured this was close enough, so I undid the wrappings this morning. It had this cereal mixture in it. I guess it must be some creation of Boston shopkeepers."

"What else did he send?' Jack asked.

"Jack, that's not nice," Hannah scolded.

Kim looked at Jack. He was a good and honest man, but he was also very hungry.

"Just a few things," Kim said. "I'm going to share them with everyone, but the cereal is for Hannah."

"Of course," said Jack, looking embarrassed.

Kim walked back to the campfire slowly. Hunger and fatigue and worry had made them all into people they weren't before. She'd often wondered how civilized she truly was, and now she found herself very tempted to go off somewhere with her bag of goodies and eat them all herself. She wasn't going to do that. Her guilt would be worse than her hunger... but the thought of a chocolate bar right now made her stomach leap.

Chapter 7

A Message

"**K**im."

Kim turned as Marc walked into the clearing carrying two wooden boxes with telegraph keys attached to the top. She glanced curiously at the second box and telegraph key and at Marc, smiling smugly. The telegraph key was one he used with his HW-9, but now it appeared to be battle-scarred as though it had been made with spare parts. *What did he do to it?* she wondered. *Bash it with rocks?*

"I think we're about ready to have a little demonstration," he said.

Benjamin Fuller, followed by several of the men, walked into the clearing, glancing suspiciously at Marc's boxes. James Dearborn laughed.

"Better watch out he doesn't blow us up. Might be gunpowder in those."

"It's explosive all right," Marc said. "An idea so powerful it will change the world."

The men grew silent and the women who were outside their wagons gathered behind the men.

"What we have here," said Marc setting one box with its telegraph key on a tree stump, "is a way to communicate with each other. I don't know how many of you have read about what Samuel F.B. Morse is demonstrating back east, but he..."

"A lot of tom foolery, that's what it is," James Dearborn interrupted.

"He's shown that people can communicate via the wonders of electrical current. You do believe in electricity, don't you?" Marc asked the people who stared at him silently.

"This box contains a battery," Marc said pointing to the black box. "I've sealed it up so as not to disturb it."

"What's in it?" Hannah's husband, Jack, asked.

"Well there are many kinds of batteries – devices for making electrical energy. This particular one is salt water and copper and steel in a glass jar."

"Why have you got it hidden?"Thomas Amalind asked suspiciously.

"Thomas, you've all seen my battery inventions. I've been working on them ever since we started on the trip," Marc answered.

"But you never said they worked," Thomas said.

"That's because I was doing something wrong with the way the wire passes through the electro-magnetic coil…"

"Through the what?"Emil scoffed.

"A coil of iron wrapped with wire. It becomes a magnet which operates this telegraph key with charges of electricity. See…" Marc said, pushing the key down, hoping that the nail attached to the bottom of it extending through the hole in the box was properly depressing one of the buttons on the touch tone pad of his radio inside.

He breathed a sigh of relief when the audible tone caught the attention of the group.

"Now," Marc said somewhat dramatically as he stretched a wire from one wooden box to the other ten feet away, "we can send a message from one to the other."

With that, Marc depressed the key on the telegraph key and watched the faces of the men and women as the tone was heard coming from that box and also from the one sitting a distance a way.

"Morse has known for some time that you could do that," Marc said. "But what's kind of new is the fact that you can do it without a wire."

Kim watched the people carefully. If any of them read the news, they would know that no one had been successful with wireless communication… yet. But Marc was banking on the fact that this group was not well read. In fact, many of them didn't know how to read. Marc continued on with his demonstration, enjoying the expressions of wonder on the people's faces as he told him that some inventors were theorizing that someday people would be able to talk to each other from different parts of the world.

Thomas Amalind, already drunk at 11 in the morning, broke into laughter so intense at that statement that Marc had to wait for him to stop.

"Kim," Marc said quietly. "Would you help me?"

"Certainly," she said, stepping forward and smiling at the group.

"Kimberly and I both have learned the code that Morse is using for messages. Until people figure out a way to send their actual voices, code will have to do."

"Send their voices?" Thomas Amalind thought that statement was hilarious. He laughed heartily, inspiring chuckles in the others. Marc glared at him and then at James Dearborn who repeated the statement again. "Send their voices?" Benjamin Fuller seemed to think he should say it a third time. "Send their voices?" The wagon master laughed and laughed until his laughter turned into a fit of coughing. Marc and Kim waited patiently for them to quiet.

"Kim will stay here while I go into the woods a distance away. Would someone like to go with me?" Marc asked, raising his voice above the noise of the men.

"I will," Emil said, stepping forward.

Kim waited nervously as Marc and Emil disappeared into a clump of brush beyond their encampment. The box holding the telegraph key gave one beep indicating that Marc was ready. Kim turned to Benjamin Fuller.

"What would you like to say to them?" she asked.

Benjamin wiped the tears from his eyes and smiled.

"Ask them who the greatest American was or is?"

Kim sent the message rapidly and listened to the return beeping.

"There seems to be some disagreement, sir," she said politely. "Emil says George Washington; Marc says Benjamin Franklin."

"Well at least he got the first name right," Thomas joked, poking Benjamin in the ribs.

"She's probably just making that up," someone else suggested.

"Call them back and ask them," Kim said quietly.

When Marc and Emil returned, that was exactly what Benjamin Fuller did. His mouth dropped open when Emil repeated his message word for word and then immediately wanted another demonstration.

Marc agreed to just one more but said that he had to be careful to save his batteries. Kim knew it wasn't the make-believe batteries of salt water and metal he was referring to, but the tiny ones inside the two meter rig.

"You said you were going to re-charge them with that contraption you put on top of our wagon," Emil said, laughing. "Charge them from the sun."

Again, Marc and Kim waited for the laughter to die down before asking if anyone else wanted to try sending a message. They did. This time, one of the women asked the question of Benjamin who had walked out of sight with Marc. She asked him details about the exact time and departure of their wagon train from Missouri, and the people gasped in amazement when the correct answer came back.

"You see," said Marc later when they were all gathered around the campsite. "We can use this sparingly as a scouting device. I can go ahead with the telegraph to make sure the trail ahead is passable before we try to move the wagons through. I'll radio... I mean, I'll send the information back to Kim and if everything's clear ahead, you can start moving. That will save us a lot of time waiting for scouts to come back. It will be that much sooner that we get to the Willamette Valley," he said, looking at Jack. "And that much sooner that people who are ailing, like Jack's wife, can get to a doctor."

"We were only a hundred feet apart. How long does it take for a message to come back from say a mile?" Emil said.

"I think this device will work up to several miles," Marc said. "And the message comes back instantly, no matter how far apart we are."

At that, the men laughed again, but Benjamin Fuller looked thoughtful. The burden of getting the wagons through was on his shoulders and at this point, he needed help. He coughed again and whispered something to James Dearborn.

They moved the wagons out a little after noon. It was too late to attempt to go down the path that led to the valley, so they agreed to camp just at the beginning of the descent. As suggested, Marc rode ahead with two other men. When Benjamin Fuller asked who wanted to go with Marc, Robert Nelson and Mitchell Copeland, two of Marc's young bachelor friends immediately volunteered. They looked disappointed when Marc turned to James Dearborn and Emil Burchart and politely asked them if they'd accompany him.

"You know a lot more about the trails than I do," Marc said, "and any decisions that have to be made... I'd just feel better if you were along."

In truth, the older men didn't know any more about the trail ahead than the younger ones. This was a first for all of them, but Kim knew Marc was trying to gain some credibility with the senior members of the group.

Even though the pace for the wagons that day was fairly easy, there was very little visiting among the women. Kim poked her head into Hannah's wagon every chance she got, but the young mother was always asleep. The baby was beginning to whimper and Kim worried that it was probably getting plenty hungry in spite of the sugar water Adeline had fixed up for it earlier.

Bobby, strangely quiet, walked beside Kim behind Adeline's wagon.

"Are you tired?" Kim asked him.

He shook his head, staring at the ground his small worn boots scuffed along.

"You can ride, you know. You don't weigh very much."

"I saw this show on T.V. once," he said quietly.

"And?" Kim questioned.

"My parents were watching it. They thought I was sleeping, but I wasn't."

"What was it about?"

"Some people going over mountains in wagons," Bobby said, his lower lip quivering.

"Where were they going?" Kim asked.

"I don't know. There was lots of snow and all the people were hungry."

Kim caught her breath. She was afraid she knew the rest of this story.

"Were they called the Donner party?" she asked him.

Bobby nodded, kicking at the dirt.

"That's not going to happen to us, Bobby. Those people were going to California. We're going to Oregon," she said with finality as though that could make a difference.

"Oh," he said sounding relieved. "I guess I want to ride a while."

Kim lifted him in the back of the wagon where he promptly lay down on some quilts and curled up on his side, his thumb in his mouth. As the afternoon wore on, she tried not to think about the ache in her legs and feet. She looked over at the other women and men following behind their wagons. All were silent, staring ahead, absorbed in their own thoughts. Kim thought back to the joyful, almost party-like atmosphere of the early days on the trail (the fact that she could remember these things no longer surprised her).

She reached down into her pocket and pulled her watch up to the edge so she could see it. Three o'clock. She'd found the watch in her pocket the same day she discovered the Penicillin. People in the wagon train certainly had timepieces, but nobody had a Timex, so Kim had hidden it along with her other 20th century inventions. At 3:30, Marc was supposed to try the first long distance radio contact with her. Hopefully, by then, he and Emil and James would have decided on the easiest way down Ladd Canyon Hill into the Grande Ronde Valley. Tales passed back from other emigrants emphasized the steepness of the descent. It was important to see the actual path before committing the wagons.

At 3:30, Kim had the now awake Bobby hand her the telegraph box. With a poke of the nail, she turned the two meter rig on inside it and held the box up to her ear, while continuing to walk. Several of the other men walked back to her and watched skeptically as the series of beeping dots and dashes sounded from the box.

Kim sent a return message on the telegraph key and then turned to the men.

"He says it's very difficult but we can do it. As soon as we go over the ridge there's a Y in the path. He says we won't see it unless we look hard for it. We should go to the left. That's a little less steep. They're going to camp up there and see if they can find a deer so we'll have venison tomorrow."

Sixty-year old Thomas Amalind stared at her and Kim felt her cheeks redden. He was Kim's least favorite person in the entire wagon train. No one was sure where he was getting his liquor, but there was widespread suspicion that he was stealing supplies from the wagons and swapping them for alcohol at the various trading stations they'd passed through. Today, he was even more obnoxious than usual. It was amazing to her that the group tolerated his behavior at all, but apparently he had some financial connection with the settlers already in the Willamette Valley. It was Thomas who had promised the group that his cousin Henry was already staking out land claims for them.

"Old Thomas is going to take good care of you folks," he told them everytime he stumbled out of his wagon drunk. But now, he looked at Kim with narrowed eyes and said, "That thing looks like some sort of witchcraft to me. If she says go left, I say we should go right."

Kim tried not to let her anger show. She'd wondered how long it would take before someone would be afraid of communication instead of grateful for the opportunity it presented.

"It's not witchcraft, Mr. Amalind," Kim assured him. "If you read the newspaper, you'd know that similar devices are in use back on the East Coast."

She regretted the words the minute they were out of her mouth. Thomas couldn't read. He snapped back at her.

"Where I come from, young ladies behave like young ladies. They don't talk back to their elders."

He stalked off angrily. Kim watched the others anxiously but there was little comment among them.

They made camp at dusk and Grayson Hodges and Nigel Harrington came back triumphantly with a string of trout from fishing in a nearby stream. Kim marveled at the discipline of the women as they made the fire and waited for the fish to cook. Her mouth watered as she smelled it. No one would eat until it had been divided equally and they had stood around the campfire with their heads bowed for the evening prayer.

After supper, Kim went to Hannah and Jack's wagon where Hannah was trying without results to nurse young Kimberly. The baby cried and flailed her small arms around.

Kim took her young namesake and rocked her back and forth. Adeline had fixed another bottle of warm sugar water and this time the baby sucked on it eagerly. That would keep her alive for a little while but if Hannah wasn't able to feed her soon, Kim didn't know what they would do. She thought of the dead Bessie, the patient brown and white cow who had so faithfully provided them all with rich, warm milk each day until she'd drowned. No wonder the wagon trains who planned more carefully took large herds of cattle with them.

Marc had radioed her a second time just before dinner reporting that there was no sign of the Olson train ahead of them. With the delays they'd had in the last week, the Olsons were probably already to the Columbia and well on their way to reaching their destination.

Jack climbed into the wagon and Kim handed him his daughter.

"Marc says they've seen several deer. They'll get one at day-break. I just know they will, and tomorrow I'll help make a stew for Hannah. That will make her strong," Kim promised Jack.

Jack tried to smile but concern filled his face. Hannah was asleep again, her cheeks slightly flushed. Kim backed out of the wagon and shivered from the cold and fatigue as she walked back to the Burchart wagon. Bobby's head popped up over the edge.

"Tell me a story, Kim," he begged.

Kim sighed and climbed in.

"Okay, what do you want to hear?"

"Power Rangers," Bobby said.

Kim shook her head no as she looked over at Adeline sitting on the floor writing in her diary by candlelight.

"How about one about a young Viking warrior named Robert the Strong?" she suggested.

"Okay," Bobby said, snuggling down happily in his quilts.

Without looking up, Adeline handed Kim her diary.

"And as soon as you're done with your story telling, remember you have two days journaling to do."

"Yes, of course," Kim said, taking the book.

Adeline's Diary

October 24, 1845.

Dear Diary:

What a day this has been! It began with the birth of a new member of this expedition to Oregon. Kimberly Ann Worth was born this morning at daybreak. The joy of having a new life among us is tempered with the knowledge that her mother is very weak. I'm fearful that neither mother nor child will survive. May the Good Lord bless them.

Since everyone had been awake most of the night, we did not begin traveling until midday. Our morning was filled with chores but also with a most unusual event. Marcus and Kimberly showed us an electrical contraption that makes it possible for people a distance away from each other to talk. Just imagine! I'm still not sure that it's not some trick — those two seem stranger every day, but the men seemed to believe it, and now Marcus and my Emil and James have gone on ahead. Already, they have "talked" if you could call those odd-sounding beeps "talking" to us twice, telling what lies ahead on the trail.

As I write this, Kimberly is inventing some outlandish tale about Viking warriors for Robert. What an imagination that girl has. She really is a good-natured sort and she was very helpful to Hannah during her birthing pains, but I think she's in for a big surprise if she believes her kind of bold behavior — talking back to the men and all — will be suitable for a lady in Oregon.

I'm waiting for her to write in her journal and now she's gone and dozed off. Well, she's not going to get away with that. There are things we do each day and she needs to know that.

Chapter 8

Going down the Mountain

When Kim awoke at first light, she was more than a little annoyed to have Adeline hand her the diary. Usually, she was up and dressed and out of the wagon before the older woman stirred, but not today. *Why I bet she's been lying there just waiting for me to wake up so I could finish my writing.* Kim felt like a school child who has just been reprimanded in front of the class, but she didn't dare argue with Adeline. Quickly, she took the book and sat near the wagon opening.

Dear Diary, Kim wrote, trying desperately to think of something to write that would entertain Adeline and at the same time give her a sense of satisfaction that the old woman wasn't getting the best of her.

Yesterday was a long day but it ended or rather I should say began with the birth of a new child. What a precious gift. Hannah and Jack are so joyful. Now there will be three people in their family to share in the wonderful life that lies ahead for them in Oregon.

I was so tired after being up all night that I could scarcely keep my eyes open while we walked ahead to this camping place. Kim paused to think and then smiled mischievously. *If it hadn't been for what Marissa told me about Carolyn, I think I would have fallen over in my tracks. Could it be true, dear diary? Such a dreadful thing. I won't even dignify such a rumor by putting it on paper.*

It's time to get ready for the journey ahead today. I must look in on little Kimberly and help Adeline to get the wagon ready. Adeline is such a kind person. I am so grateful to her for all she's done and for allowing me to journey to Oregon in their wagon.

By tonight, we shall all be safe on the floor of the Grande Ronde Valley and I will be able to hear from Marcus the adventures that he has had.

Kim smiled as she reached up to put the diary back on its shelf. This ought to drive Adeline wild with curiosity. Marissa and Carolyn were two of her closest friends. She would never dream of questioning them about a secret, but the idea that they had one and hadn't shared it with her would keep her mind busy all day.

Once they were on the road, Kim had little time to think about her prank. For the first two hours, the animals labored to pull the wagons up the hills. Every person except Hannah walked and over particularly rough spots, the men hung on to the animals' pulling harnesses and pulled with them.

At the top of the ridge, they rested. Down below them lay the valley, but the sight of the steep trail down to it was frightening. Slowly, they began the descent. The oxen braced their feet and stopped, sending rocks skidding ahead of them. The men fastened chains around trees to act as brakes for the wagons.

Inch by inch, they moved down the mountainside, the frightened eyes of the animals matching those of their owners. At one point, the people stopped to look over the edge where a wagon from an earlier train lay smashed to pieces at the bottom.

The wagons bounced and crashed into potholes, and Kim tried not to think of the pain those motions were causing Hannah. Kim held Bobby's hand and concentrated on small measures of progress.

"Look at that big boulder down there," she said pointing to a huge overhang 100 feet beyond them. "Let's play a game and pretend that it's as far as we have to go."

The little boy nodded and when they reached the place, he shouted, "We made it!" which caused some of the others to turn and stare.

"We did make that goal but now we have to pick another," Kim said. "How about that broken tree growing out of the side of the mountain?"

65

Landmark by landmark, they celebrated their progress, and when they finally reached the bottom, Bobby let out a big whoop and said, "That was fun."

Kim hugged him before he ran off to play with the other children romping in the tall grass. Marc worked with the men to unhitch all the animals and let them graze the tall grass to fill their bellies. When he was done helping arrange the wagons for the night, Marc walked over to Kim. He bent down and kissed her.

"Marc," she whispered. "Emil is staring at us."

"I don't care," he said. "I've been thinking about you all day and worrying that one of the wagons would crash into you or something."

"We were fine, but if that was the easy route down, I sure wouldn't have wanted to be on the hard one."

"Well, I think our little radio communication impressed them. At least, they listened to what we had to say."

"Thomas didn't," Kim told him. "In fact, he tried his darnedest to convince people to do exactly the opposite, but Benjamin Fuller said we would do what you advised."

"I think Emil likes me a little better now. We chatted about building houses all day. Seems he's promised Adeline a home bigger than she had in Missouri."

Kim giggled.

"What's so funny?"

"Oh nothing, just a little trick I'm playing on Adeline."

There was no time to tell him more as a couple of the men shouted for Marc to come help with a damaged wagon shaft and he went running. Kim walked over to help prepare the evening meal. With the animals content and the fire blazing, life seemed hopeful once again.

Emil, standing by his wife, looked around at the valley surrounded by mountains and said, "I could live here."

Adeline gave him a worried frown. Except for a few trappers cabins, the valley was unsettled. Her sister and brother-in-law with their two daughters had emigrated to the Willamette

Valley a year earlier. Kim knew Adeline was counting the days until she could be with them again, but obedient wife that she was, she didn't say anything to contradict her husband in public. What might be said in the privacy of the wagon was another matter.

The bacon grease was long gone, but the women used some of the beef fat to fry up some cornmeal cakes to accompany the fresh venison and trout the men had brought in. Kim carried a plate of food to Hannah who was trying to nurse the whimpering baby Kimberly in vain.

"I don't seem to have any milk," she told Kim weakly. "I don't know what's wrong; I just don't feel well."

Adeline had been forcing Hannah to drink water all day long to combat dehydration from the blood loss she'd suffered during the difficult birth. Kim looked at the young woman's cheeks, flushed even more than they'd been this morning, and reached out to feel them. Hannah felt as though she were burning up. *She's got an infection,* Kim thought, suddenly remembering the Penicillin tablets hidden away in a corner of the wagon. *Would they make her well? Once the pills were gone, they were gone. What about Benjamin Fuller who had been coughing more intensely each day? Was he developing pneumonia?*

Kim pondered these and other unanswerable questions as she walked around the perimeter of the encampment to the wagon of Susan and Grayson Hodges. At age 32, Susan was the only other nursing mother in the group. She had lost three babies to various maladies before giving birth to young Andrew at the beginning of the trip. Susan guarded his health with zeal and Grayson often gave her a portion of his food to ensure that she would keep on producing milk for their young growing son. Kim had no idea how she would answer what she was going to ask her, but for Hannah and Kimberly's sake, she had to try.

"I feel very sorry for her. I certainly do," said Susan clutching the wiggly Andrew to her with her own thin arms.

She looked at her husband who didn't say anything.

"It's just until Hannah gets her own milk," Kim said.

Silence and then.

"Maybe she never will. She's very sick, I've heard," said Susan. "What if she dies? What then?"

She kissed the top of Andrew's head.

"I can't nurse two babies. I barely have enough for him."

Kim nodded sadly and turned to leave. There was a rustling behind her and when she turned, she saw Susan climbing down from the wagon. The two of them walked without speaking a word to Hannah's wagon.

"Thank you," Kim said to her as she climbed in, but Susan ignored her.

And she ignored Hannah's relieved greeting too. Susan crouched on the floor silently.

"Susan's going to nurse Kimberly for you," Kim told her, gently taking the tiny baby from its blanket on the floor beside Hannah.

Hannah's feverish eyes watched Susan put the baby to her breast.

"It's just for a couple of days," Kim told Hannah, "until you get to feeling better."

Hannah lay silent, tears in her eyes. Susan finished feeding the baby and when it fell asleep in her arms, she handed her back without a word and left the wagon.

"I was hoping there would be someone in this valley with a milk cow," Kim told Marc after dinner as they walked along the edge of the wagons. He carried his back pack, hidden under a burlap bag, and while they stopped to talk, he placed it behind a wagon wheel.

"I think that comes a few years later. I guess I should have paid more attention in history class," he told her, looking desolately at the ground.

"We are history class," Kim said.

They were silent as they walked along, their long friendship communicating for them without words.

"Do you think Hannah will live?" he asked her.

"I don't know. I've been wondering all afternoon if I should give her the Penicillin."

"I had forgotten you had that. It couldn't hurt to try."

"Marc, what about Benjamin Fuller? I think he has pneumonia."

"What about half to each?" Marc suggested.

"It doesn't work that way. If you don't take enough to kill off the bacteria, it won't do any good. I have to choose."

"I can't help you with that one," Marc said. "They're your pills. You decide."

There was an abruptness to his tone that was unusual for Marc. Kim looked at him with concern, but he was busy staring at the fire, his face dark with sadness. Kim touched his arm gently.

"What are you thinking?"

He shook his head, refusing to answer.

"Look Marc. I'm not very happy about this whole scene either, but I guess we've just got to go along with whatever cosmic trick we've become part of. You and I are the same, aren't we?"

"Sure," he said, but his words belied his expression. The two of them leaned against the wagon, watching the flickering of the campfire reach toward the sky. The clouds of yesterday had cleared late in the afternoon, and while it was chilly now in the evening, it wasn't as cold as it had been the night before. Maybe the weather was going to hold off for them.

Marc reached down and picked up his pack.

Kim glanced around them.

"After what Thomas said this morning, I think we need to be really careful not to let anyone see our other stuff."

"Right. I'll keep the two meter rigs so we can continue our wireless hoax, but I'm going to dump the HW-9 in the woods tonight. It's useless to us now."

"You really are depressed, aren't you?"

"What's the use of hanging on to something that might cause more suspicion if anyone finds it."

"This is not the Marc I know."

"Yeah, well this isn't the world I know."

69

Kim watched him as he walked away. Throughout this ordeal, Marc had been her anchor. She didn't know what she'd do if he was slipping away. For the next two hours as they made dinner and had evening prayers, Kim looked around anxiously for Marc. He was nowhere to be seen.

At nightfall, Kim walked over to the Harrington wagon to retrieve Bobby who was playing a game with Jasper. She brought him back and tucked him into bed and then lit a candle. She was in no mood to do anything, but she knew Adeline would be there soon and begin pestering her about the diary. She grabbed the small book from the shelf. She'd take care of this chore and then she could devote her thoughts to a way to cheer up Marc. She paused, pen in hand, over the page and then she gave a slight smile.

Dear Diary

I found out something today that is just about to drive me insane. Not only are Carolyn and Marissa in on the secret, but Mary Simmons knows too. I wouldn't have dreamed that they'd tell her. It makes me wonder how they can talk and carry on normally during the day knowing the dreadful facts that they do. Someday, dear diary, I won't be able to contain myself and then I will have to tell you. For the moment, though, I am working hard on improving my self control as Adeline tells me it is one of the virtues that a woman should have. So for tonight, at least, their secret is safe.

Kim wrote on, telling of the details of the descent down the hills and of her concern for Hannah. Out of the corner of her eye, she could see Adeline, looking up occasionally from her own journal writing to sneak a peek over at Kim's to see how much of the page she had covered.

I bet she can hardly wait until I leave the wagon each morning, Kim thought forcing back a smile. With a yawn, she handed her diary to Adeline to place up on the shelf with her own, and then she climbed into the bed quilts.

Kim lay awake long after Adeline and Bobby's soft snoring filled the wagon. She willed her spirit to be with Marc. Although his moodiness worried her, she trusted in his overall stability to make the best of this situation. Maybe he was right.

If they had to live in the past, it was better to get rid of things that would remind them of all they had left behind. But still she couldn't imagine him abandoning his HW-9. For him to give up on communications would be like Benjamin Fuller to give up on leading the wagon to the Willamette Valley.

For the moment, her thoughts turned to the tall, lean man who had been their able leader so far. He had started coughing somewhere in Wyoming, and tonight when he'd walked past her, she noticed his shoulders were hunched forward like he was struggling to breathe. Two candidates for her magic white pills. Would there be more before their trek was ended? And what of the years to come? How many opportunities would there be to use the life-giving medicine?

****

Deep in a brushy area, far from the camp, Marc sat on a boulder, his HW-9 set up on the ground in front of him. He'd decided to fire it up one last time, so he would have the memory of its glowing dials. Perhaps he'd send a message into space. Maybe it would float around and around – the kind of thing he'd read about in science fiction books – and someday, centuries from now, some ham radio operator would hear the last transmission from KA7ITR.

The antenna, strung to a shrub some distance away, swayed in the breeze, as Marc turned his radio on and began to transmit. *Hello anyone from KA7ITR. My rig is an HW-9 and my antenna is a piece of wire run between two mesquite bushes.* He sent the same message over and over, deciding not to tell what his plight was. After all, no one would ever hear this anyway. It was better just to pretend it was a normal communication and that he was giving the standard information that amateur operators exchanged. He'd switch the transceiver to receive and then he'd walk away, leaving the rig set up that way. If the metal survived, it'd give some student archaeologist a good find in the twentieth century.

71

Adeline's Diary

October 25, 1845

Dear Diary:

Tomorrow we will cross the valley and the day after, we will begin the final part of our journey. If we can survive our travels through the Blue Mountains, and God has brought us this far — why doubt the rest? — we will soon reach the magnificent Columbia River. Emil spoke today about wanting to stay here in this valley. Perhaps if we were younger, it would be an adventure, but now all I can think of is being reunited with my friends and relatives.

A disturbing note. Kimberly has written of strange secrets among the women of our group. I can not believe that any of them would hide a confidence from me, so I think that possibly Kimberly is imagining all of this. What a strange child she is.

CHAPTER 9

How Marc Spent the Night

An hour or so before dawn, Kim drifted off into a dreamless sleep only to be interrupted by Benjamin Fuller's hoarse voice yelling "Turn out, Turn out!"

She woke up to find that she was alone in the wagon. Hurriedly, she dressed and fumbled around in the bottom of the chest to find another granola bar. There were only three left. She unwrapped it, hid the wrapper, and carried it to the fire to mix with hot water. Benjamin was pacing back and forth, worrying that people weren't getting ready fast enough for the day's journey ahead. His cough, more like a bark now, cut through Kim's consciousness.

She was relieved to see Marc helping Alexander Malby hooking his oxen up to a wagon. Marc saw her and waved. Apparently whatever he had done in the woods had given him peace. Now they could look to the future.

May Belle Fuller stopped Kim as she was mixing hot water with the granola bars for Hannah's breakfast.

"My husband is very ill," she said.

"Yes, I know," Kim said. "I could hear his coughing during the night."

"Where did you get that cereal?"

"I thought everyone knew," Kim explained. "My uncle sent me some special goods from a store in Boston. I brought them along and was saving them, but Hannah needs them more than I do."

"My husband has to be kept strong," May Belle said staring at Kim.

The woman's stare made Kim uneasy, and she answered quickly.

"Of course he does. Hopefully, the meat we've been eating and what the men hope to shoot today will strengthen him."

Without waiting for her to say more, Kim moved away toward Hannah's wagon.

If anything, Hannah seemed worse this morning, but Kim greeted her with a warm smile. A worried Susan sat on a barrel next to Hannah nursing Kimberly.

"Here's your cereal, Hannah," she said kneeling down beside the sick woman. Susan finished with the baby and, just as she'd done the night before, laid her down beside Hannah and left the wagon without a word.

"I don't feel hungry," Hannah said, her face flushed with fever.

Kim raised a spoonful of the cereal up to her mouth. In the center of the glob of moistened granola was a white pill. Hannah stared down at it.

"It's some special medicine my uncle gave me," Kim said. "You must swallow it."

Obediently, Hannah opened her mouth.

"If I die, Kimberly, will you make sure Susan keeps on nursing the baby?"

"You're not going to die, Hannah," Kim said sternly. "I've brought you a glass of water and I want you to drink all of it even if you don't want it."

Hannah seemed startled by the authority in Kim's voice, but she allowed Kim to tilt the glass so she could take a sip.

"I'll be back in a little while. You rest."

Hannah closed her eyes and Kim climbed out of the wagon. She walked toward Adeline's wagon, trying not to think of the long walk ahead. To her surprise, several of the women were gathered around the rear of the wagon and Kim's trunk was on the ground, the lid flung open with the wedding dress draped over it.

"What are you doing?" Kim yelled as she ran toward them.

Kim and Marc had been careful to hide their backpacks of radio parts, but the remnants of her foodstuffs were still in the bottom of the trunk... or at least they had been. Now they were strewn on the ground: Marc's granola bars, plastic baggies of trail mix and a plastic container of dried soup. Somehow, they hadn't found the chocolate bars which Kim had moved over to her sleeping bag hidden in the corner.

May Belle was in the middle of the women and she was holding up each item. She looked at the plastic container curiously.

"I've never seen anything like this," she said accusingly.

"Mrs. Fuller, there're probably a lot of things you haven't seen," Kim said.

The wife of the wagon train's leader turned on her angrily.

"Thomas told me you were insolent. I thought it was just his liquor talking, but perhaps he was correct."

She lifted the lid from the container and sniffed it.

"It's dried soup."

"Dried? You can't dry soup."

"There's a process for taking the liquid out of it... sort of like you make jerked meat," Kim said.

"You certainly know a lot for one so young. Did this come from that famous uncle of yours, too?" May Belle asked.

"Yes, it did. And if you add some hot water to it, it might help your husband to get rid of that cough."

"I thought you were saving everything for your friend, Hannah."

"Hannah will be all right without the soup."

At that, the women exchanged glances. Although they didn't say it aloud, everyone of them believed Hannah would be dead before the week was over.

Mary Simmons picked up one of the soup mixes and sniffed it appreciatively.

"Go on, take it. Take it all, if you want. If I had wanted to eat it, I already would have. I was saving it for a celebration when we reach the Columbia," Kim told them scooping up her wedding dress.

The women, all except Adeline, hesitated just a minute and then snatched the remnants of Kim's foodstuffs. They ran back to their wagons to get ready for the moving out onto the trail.

With tears in her eyes, Kim brushed the dust from the hem of her wedding dress and folded it back into the trunk. Silently, Adeline helped her lift it back in the trunk and place the trunk in the wagon. Kim stood still, expecting Adeline to comfort her for the scene that had just occurred, but Adeline climbed up in the wagon and took the reins without a word.

****

Marc whistled as he walked through the circle of wagons to his horse, Rosie. Thomas Amalind looked at him with scorn.

"Not much to be whistling about is there, boy?"

Marc smiled at him and ignored the comment. He wasn't about to get into it with Thomas, but he wouldn't let the man dampen his mood either. For the first time since this whole bizarre thing had begun, he felt a ray of hope. He looked over at Kim emerging from Hannah and Jack's wagon. The two of them deliberately altered their paths so they would pass close together. Kim greeted him with tears in her eyes.

"What's the matter?"

"I thought about what you said," Kim said. "You're right. We have to abandon the past and get on with this future, and I was all set to do just that until this morning. Those awful women dumped my wedding dress out on the ground while they searched through my things."

Marc looked at her sympathetically, but he was smiling when he leaned to whisper something.

"Well don't think about that, Kim. Think about this instead. Something happened last night. I still have the HW-9. It's hidden in Grayson's wagon."

"What?"

"I was just ready to turn it off and walk away and I heard some static."

"Static?"

"Yes and maybe something else, but I'm not sure. All I can tell you is that I can hardly wait for tonight."

With that, he smiled at her and ran to help Charles Harley and Grayson Hodges harness a team and check the wheels for readiness.

Grayson looked at him but didn't say anything. Marc usually slept next to him near the campfire at night and he knew Marc had left shortly after dark. Perhaps he was off with Kimberly, but he really doubted that she would have been able to sneak off under the eagle eye of Adeline. There was something strange about those two young folks. For the last few days, they had just seemed different. Hard to pinpoint, but something about them made him feel uneasy, and he certainly didn't like the pressure the girl had put on his wife to nurse Hannah's baby. That was something Susan should have decided – the request shouldn't have been made by an outsider. He just hoped that Susan's generosity wouldn't cost their little Andrew any of his strength.

Marc kept his head down and worked hard even though he was dying to go tell Kim the rest of the story – the outlandish theory that had surfaced in his brain at dawn this morning. Soon the wagons were lined up and the signal to move out was given. Marc tied his horse to the back of the Hodges wagon.

Today, they were just going to be traveling across the Grande Ronde Valley, perhaps 15 miles or so. The ascent up the Blue Mountains would begin tomorrow. The horses were plenty tired so the men, all except Benjamin Fuller who had finally consented to lie down in their wagon for the day, would walk in hopes that they would be refreshed enough for the scouting and hunting forays they needed to do tomorrow.

Bobby sat in the back of Adeline and Emil's wagon, swinging his legs and listening to Kim who was trying to invent a story to entertain him.

"How big was the monster?" Bobby asked.

"Bigger than any monster the world had ever seen"

"Bigger than a prairie schooner?"

"Yes, bigger than that."

"Bigger than a house?"

"Yes, bigger than a house."

"Bigger than a space shuttle?" Bobby asked and then clapped his hand over his mouth, giggling. He had decided that knowing about things the others didn't was a fun game, and Kim had yet to convince him otherwise.

"End of story," she said abruptly.

The only way she could make him be careful of what he said at all was simply to stop talking to him when he disobeyed the rules about not mentioning the future. Bobby pouted and scrambled back in the wagon.

****

They rested briefly at noon and then pressed on, desperately trying to make up time. At four, the animals had to have rest. The wagons came to a halt and the draft animals were set loose to graze the lush valley grass. Several of the men had gone ahead to hunt earlier in the afternoon, and now they came back carrying an assortment of small game. Kim watched the gray clouds scudding in over the mountains.

All of the firewood they gathered seemed to be wet and the women struggled to get a fire going. Marc brought an armload of brush and wood and placed it carefully on the fire. No one looked up as he walked by; in fact, Kim keenly felt that the group was intentionally isolating the two of them ever since the food incident this morning. It made her angry and afraid at the same time.

At last, the fire was going and meat was placed on it to roast. At a small trading station in the east part of the valley, the group had bought some flour at sixty cents a pound, and now the women mixed it into kind of a flat biscuit to serve with the meat. Benjamin Fuller did not appear for dinner and May Belle, with an accusing glance at Kim, carried a plate of food to the wagon where he lay resting.

Kim chopped up some meat and biscuit and added hot water to make a bowl of stew. To her surprise, Hannah was sitting up. Kim wondered if it was her imagination that she looked a little less flushed. Susan must have already been there to feed the baby because little Kimberly was sound asleep with a contented peacefulness on her face.

"I drank all the water just like you said," Hannah told Kim as she climbed into the wagon.

"Good. Here's another glass and here's another of these white pills." Kim had given her two that morning and one at noon.

"Are those what's making me feel better?" Hannah asked. "Because I do think I feel a bit better."

"Yes,"Kim said as she watched Hannah swallow the pill and start to eat the stew.

"Maybe you should give some to Mr. Fuller too,"said Hannah. "Jack says he's very ill."

"There's only enough for one person," Kim told her.

"Oh,"Hannah said, looking somberly at Kim. "And you chose me?"

"I thought they would work better on the kind of illness you have," Kim said, and then lowering her voice, she added, "but it might be best if you didn't tell anyone about the medicine."

Hannah considered this as she ate her stew silently. When Kim got ready to leave, she reached out and touched Kim on the sleeve.

"Thank you," she said softly.

Kim walked quietly back to the group. She hoped Hannah would keep the secret of the little white pills to herself because if it ever came out that she had chosen the young mother over the group leader, she didn't know what would happen. And she doubted that they'd believe that the way Kim made the decision after an agonizing night of debate was to simply flip a coin... even though it was the truth.

CHAPTER 10

To Go Or Stay

T he night passed. Kim woke up twice, wondering if Marc had been able to try his radio transmission again. She had no idea why hearing static had raised his spirits so much, but she was grateful for anything that made him optimistic.

The camp got up to pounding rain. Scurrying back and forth, they carried out their chores as usual although breakfast was a hurried affair eaten in the wagons. Kim wrapped a wool cloak around her and sat on the floor of the wagon with Bobby and Adeline. Emil stayed with a group of men sitting by the fire, despite the rain. As they ate, they leaned toward each other, deep in talk. Kim looked out of the wagon anxiously wondering where Marc was.

She finally spotted him over by the Hodges wagon inspecting a place on a wheel that had been repaired that morning.

"I'm cold," Bobby complained.

Without a word, Adeline wrapped a blanket around the boy and then continued eating silently.

"Look!" Bobby exclaimed. "Snow!"

He pointed out the wagon opening at big soft snowflakes falling from the sky.

"I remember when I was little like last year that it snowed at Christmas and me and my dad went to see Star Crusader together. It was neat..."

He stopped at Kim's expression and put his hand over his mouth.

"You're right. He does have an imagination, doesn't he?" Kim said weakly, trying to ignore Adeline's stare.

The men were leaving the campfire now and approaching the Fuller wagon. Several of them climbed in and the rest stood on the outside. Apparently, there was some sort of a discussion underway. Pretty soon, Emil came walking back. He spoke directly to Adeline, ignoring Kim's presence.

"The women are having a meeting. Best you go over to the Harrington wagon."

Adeline climbed down and walked toward the other women assembling on the far side of the clearing around Marissa Harrington. May Belle Fuller, her face expressionless, was the last to join them.

"What's going on?"

Kim turned to see Marc standing at the back of the wagon. Bobby piped up.

"I talked about a movie. I'm sorry."

Marc didn't seem to hear him. He just stood there with a big smile on his face.

"Kim, have you ever read about a phenomenon called long delayed echoes?"

"Yeah, that's where there've been a couple of cases of a signal being sent and received by someone and then later... I think the longest ever recorded was a half hour later... the signal is heard again. Isn't the theory that the echo of the radio signal just keeps on bouncing around?"

"I talked to someone last night," Marc said quietly.

"You what? In 1845? Are you going crazy, Marc?"

"Shhh," Marc cautioned her. "I set up the rig just the way I did the night before. Antenna line in the trees, ground line in the stream, you know..."

"Yeah?"

"And when I turned it on, before I even tried sending anything, here was this signal coming back to me, just beeping away. Calling me with my call letters... like he'd heard them the night before."

"You sure you weren't dreaming?" Kim asked skeptically.

Marc stopped walking for a minute and reached out and grabbed Kim's arm.

"Kim, I was not dreaming. I heard a real station, a W7DL – name is Bruce"

Kim looked at Marc, not knowing what to think.

"He was sending out a distress signal. Said he'd gone down in the Pacific."

"What?"

"Then I lost him."

Kim looked at Marc skeptically.

"Okay, let's say this long delayed echo theory is how he heard you. Now, can you tell me why we heard him?"

Marc shook his head.

"No," he said. "I can't, unless it's something like a wormhole."

"Wormhole," Kim repeated. "You mean the theory that dissimilar places of intense electromagnetic activity in time and space can be linked?"

"Yeah, something like that."

"Oh come on, Marc. That stuff only happens in movies."

Their conversation was interrupted by Jack Worth who came over to share what was happening.

"The men are voting to settle here for the winter," he said. "A lot of them think this valley is perfect."

"And live off what?" Kim asked. " It'd be one thing if we had built cabins already and had lots of supplies, but we don't. And it's getting so late, I doubt we'll see more traders coming east from the Dalles before spring. Our only chance is to get through to the Columbia."

Jack seemed slightly surprised at Kim's outburst of opinion, but he nodded his head in agreement.

"I voted no," he said, "Right now it's half and half. Benjamin Fuller is the deciding vote and he hasn't decided yet."

With a resolute set to his face, Marc walked over to the Fuller wagon. Jack followed him. Kim watched as the two of them climbed in. Kim sat in the wagon, wrapped in a blanket with Bobby and tried to entertain him with stories while her eyes remained focused on the back of the Fuller wagon.

"Don't stop now," Bobby protested when she abruptly halted her tale of dinosaurs. Marc had just emerged from the wagon and was walking to another wagon, the one belonging to the Dearborns. Kim half-heartedly played with a spinning wooden top that Bobby delighted in sending crashing into her ankles, but all the while, her eyes were focused on the wagons. Marc left the Dearborns and went to the Simmons. That didn't take long. He moved on to the Harringtons. Even quicker. Now he was at the Hodges. Apparently, whatever he was asking didn't take long to refuse.

Just as Kim decided she couldn't bear to watch anymore, he showed up at their wagon with Mitchell Copeland, one of the three single men in the wagon train.

"I want to go ahead and check out the trail over the summit," Marc told Kim. "Mitchell and Alexander have agreed to go along. "We'll send a message back at nightfall."

"You won't be back tonight?"

"I doubt it. Don't worry. I've slept in the snow before."

He turned to leave but then paused and glanced around at Mitchell who had walked out of earshot.

"If I went alone, I'd be able to take the HW-9 with me, but if I go alone, no one here will believe any message I send with our two meter wireless set up. They're still leery of that whole idea and I think the only way it has any credibility with them is if they're standing right there when I do it."

"So you want me to take the HW-9 out and contact that guy you heard?"

"Yeah, Kim. He was definitely sending a distress call."

"This is just too weird. What'd you say his name was?"

"Bruce."

Marc reached into the wagon and kissed her good-bye. Fifteen minutes later, he rode his horse by and handed her the canvas bag which held the HW-9. Kim quickly hid it under some quilts.

****

The afternoon went by quickly. Even though the vote wasn't official, the women seemed to think they were going to stay and they were already planning the cabins they would build from pine logs.

No wonder this group was late leaving from Missouri, Kim thought. *They're not thinking rationally.* Of all the wagon trains for her to be transported in time to, she wondered why it had to be this one. From what she'd heard, there were others who had left at least a month earlier, with more supplies, and a large herd of livestock which, if need be, could serve as food along the way. The idea of this tired, half-starved group dragging in logs from the forest and building cabins and then somehow living off the land until spring struck her as ridiculous. Probably some of them would make it... but at what price? She had stopped counting graves along the trail a month ago.

But at the same time that Kim was mentally criticizing the group, she also gave them credit. She wasn't sure that the 1990's Kim would have been brave enough to leave her home and set off for a faraway land with little hope of ever seeing her parents again. This group might lack planning skills, but courage they had in abundance.

Adeline, although unhappy at the vote, seemed to be intent on passing the afternoon doing needlework and when Kim engaged her in conversation, she answered briefly. Bobby left the wagon to go play with some of the other children. Kim sat on the floor and thought about the group's negative turn in emotions toward her and Marc. They were afraid. She was sure of that. It was interesting that the dangers of the land didn't frighten them as much as ideas they didn't understand. Kim gathered up her fake telegraph, slipped it into a bag, and climbed out of the wagon.

The Malbys told her they were too busy to visit. *Busy doing what?* Kim wondered as she looked at the two of them sitting on the floor of their wagon, but she didn't argue. She went on to the Harringtons where Bobby was playing with Jasper. Kim had been a favorite with their two older children, Melanie, 11 and John, 12. The kids greeted Kim warmly as she climbed into the wagon. Their parents, Marissa and Nigel, looked at her suspiciously, but they didn't tell her to leave.

Kim unwrapped the telegraph and placed it on the floor.

"The other day when Marc and I demonstrated this device, everyone seemed enthusiastic," Kim began slowly. "Now everyone treats us like we've got a disease or something. I was wondering if you could tell me why?"

Nigel and Marissa exchanged glances and then Marissa spoke.

"You've changed," Marissa said.

"Changed? How?" Kim asked.

"All that powdered soup and those strange mixtures in funny containers. Things we've never seen. And Robert here talking about things that everyone knows are silly... things like space travel."

"Haven't you ever looked at the stars and wondered what it would be like to fly to them?"

Nigel frowned.

"No," he said. "I have plenty to think about without nonsense like that."

"But not everyone thinks it's nonsense," Kim said. "There have always been people who think about all the possibilities in life. Supposing Columbus had listened to the people who thought the world was flat? Why you and I wouldn't be here traveling to Oregon, would we?"

"All this telegraph stuff with your dots and dashes and messages without wires. Some people think..." Marissa paused and looked at her husband.

"Think what, Marissa?" Kim said.

"They think the Devil lets you do it," she said staring at the floor.

"Do you believe that?" Kim asked.

"No," said Nigel. "That's why we let Bobby play with Jasper, but we do think you have too much knowledge – too much for your own good."

"You can never have too much knowledge," Kim said.

She fingered the telegraph and looked at the Harringtons.

"Pretty soon, Marc is going to send us a signal about how bad the road is out of here that leads into the mountains."

Kim reached into her pocket and produced a piece of paper with Morse Code written on it.

"When he sends it, I thought maybe you could listen too and help me read his message."

"We don't know things like that," Marissa protested.

"We could learn," John piped up.

"And I'd be happy to teach you," Kim said smiling.

At first, Marissa and Nigel seemed disapproving but as Kim taught the kids to copy code and played word games, they began to relax. At one point, when Kim said " dah dit dah dit, dit dah, dah." Marissa couldn't help herself and blurted out "Cat."

"That's right," Kim said laughing.

"How long do you suppose it will be before everyone has one of these?" Nigel asked pointing at the telegraph.

Kim thought about it for awhile.

"I kind of doubt that everyone ever will have. Not everyone is going to want to learn Morse Code, but I bet there'll be enough people who do that messages can be sent easily. And..."

She stopped herself. It was so tempting to tell them about telephones, but once she did that there'd be no stopping. If she started babbling on about television and computers and email and satellite transmissions, no telling what'd they think.

"And what, Kimberly?" Marissa asked.

"I just think that people are going to invent more and more wonderful things every year."

Outside, the men heaped wood on the fire to keep it going, and several of the women began preparing the squirrels and rabbits caught earlier in the day for supper. Kim carried the telegraph box to the clearing, hoping that others would gather around. The more people she could involve in this, perhaps the better.

86

Right on schedule, Marc's transmission came through. The Harrington children listened, trying to pick out a letter or two, but the solid copy of the code fell to Kim. She scribbled on a piece of paper and then held it up for everyone to see.

"It says they've found a path that seems passable even in this snow. Marc says we should bear left and that it's a little easier. He also says the clouds have lifted and they have a beautiful view of the Blue Mountains."

The group listened silently, and then James Dearborn snatched the piece of paper from her hand and carried it to the Fuller wagon. Kim waited anxiously, knowing that a high level conference of sorts was going on. When he didn't return, Nigel Harrington walked over and climbed into the wagon. Finally, James and Nigel came walking back, their heads bowed somberly. James turned to the group.

"Benjamin's very, very ill. He's coughing up blood. He thinks, and I believe he's right, that he's dying."

At that, there was a gasp from the people. James continued on.

"He says he's been thinking about it all day and he believes that Marcus is right... that we should go on. He said we should make plans to move out early in the morning."

"But if Mr. Fuller is too ill to be moved," protested Mary Simmons.

"He said and I'm quoting him now – 'Time is of the essence. You must move on.'"

Kim gathered up the telegraph and carried it back to their wagon. When it was bedtime, Adeline seemed a little more friendly, at least toward Bobby. She tucked him into his bedding and after she and Kim had both written in their journals, she said goodnight to Kim before pulling the quilts up around her own shoulders.

Kim lay awake, waiting until she heard the rhythmic breathing of Adeline and Bobby, indicating they were asleep. Quietly, she sat up, pulled her cloak around her, and reached under the quilts in the corner where she'd hidden the HW-9.

Clutching it under her arm, she crept out of the wagon and crouched in the shadows. She watched the figure of Nigel Harrington, assigned night watch duty, pass by and move to the far end of the wagons. The campfire was still glowing bright. She hoped that none of the men sleeping outside their tents saw her as she tiptoed toward the woods.

Adeline's Diary

October 26, 1845

Dear Diary:

Tomorrow, we move on. I cannot imagine May Belle Fuller's sorrow at knowing the journey ahead will surely kill her husband. It appears unlikely that he will live even if we stay here. We must venture forth and trust in the Lord.

I do not know what to think of Kimberly. Her unlady-like belief in scientific inventions seems so out of place for a young woman from her fine family. However, perhaps she is well-paired with Marcus as he seems to have his brain in the clouds too. I do wonder how they plan to run a business and raise a family if they spend all their time making those experiments. The men seem to believe the messages that Kimberly is receiving by that telegraph, but I still wonder if it isn't all make believe.

Tomorrow will be an interesting day.

Chapter 11

"My Name is Bruce"

The tired, worried face of Adeline stuck in Kim's mind as she made her way toward the woods. She felt a pang of guilt for writing the stories about the "secrets" in her diary. Even though the woman had no business snooping , she decided not to add to her worries by hinting that her friends were holding out on her. *Unless she really gets on my case, that is,* Kim thought.

She reached the edge of the pine trees and pulled her shawl around her tightly. The frosty wind ruffled her hair and sent shivers down her spine, making her wish for her down-filled ski jacket left somewhere back in 1998. In amongst the trees, the ground was a carpet of pine needles and Kim searched the area in front of her with her flashlight so as not to trip over branches or vines. She walked for almost a half hour before she was satisfied that she was far away from the camp to be safe.

Am I crazy or what? she thought as she set up Marc's radio and strung a hasty antenna to another tree. But what wasn't crazy in this topsy turvey world? Reason didn't seem to be a component of anything that happened. Was there some formula for making sense out of all this? Kim's thoughts raced as she connected the radio and tuned it up to listen on the frequency where Marc had heard the signal the other night. *Why am I doing this?* Kim wondered. The answer came back to her immediately. *Because it's what I would do in my former life. That's the only standard I have – to do what I would normally do.*

Kim crouched down on the ground, making a tent of her long dress around her bare legs. She put on Marc's headphones and closed her eyes, willing her ears to be keen enough to pick up the faintest of signals.

****

Adeline woke with a start. Something was wrong. She blinked several times, trying to see in the darkness of the wagon. Bobby's rhythmic breathing reassured her that he was there, but the space next to him where Kim slept was silent. Quietly, on her hands and knees, Adeline crawled between the quilts over to the side of the wagon and patted the floor. Empty!

Lighting a candle, Adeline cast its tiny light toward the shelf where the books stood. She reached for Kim's diary and flipped open the pages to tonight's entry.

October 26, 1845

Dear Diary:

Tonight, my beloved Marcus is camped in the mountains waiting for us to join him tomorrow. I am so proud of him and his bravery. If it weren't for his persistence with the telegraph, we would have no way of knowing what lies ahead.

I long for the days ahead when we will be married and can truly be together all the time.

Adeline closed the book and put it back with the others. *So that was it. Kim was off in the woods somewhere with Marcus. The story that he was sending messages was probably just a false-hood intended to make people think he was far away when really he was nearby just waiting for darkness so that he and Kimberly could sneak off.*

Adeline sat in the darkness, contemplating what to do. Perhaps she should wake the others and tell them Marcus was not to be trusted. Any message he had sent must surely be false. To go ahead on his advice was suicide. They should all just stay here. Gathering her shawl around her, she slipped from the wagon. She would go to the Malbys and let them decide if Ben Fuller should be waked.

****

Captain Bruce Thompson groaned in his sleep. His wife, Karen, was standing in the doorway smiling at him. He looked at her, taking in every detail of her beautiful face, but then suddenly she floated out of focus and then disappeared completely. Bruce opened his eyes with a start and groaned aloud. Karen was a dream. Reality was his shattered ankle, the sun glaring down on the sand beyond the canopy of trees where he lay, and the Pacific Ocean that seemed to stretch to eternity. He shaded his eyes and scanned the horizon. Not a sign of life anywhere.

He turned painfully to look behind him. The chatter of tropical birds in the trees was overwhelming, and he kept looking, expecting to find some sort of larger life – an animal, a human. The wreckage of his plane was compressed under the cover of the thick foliage of the mini-jungle.

"No sense working this out both ways." That had been the last transmission, Captain Bruce Thompson had received from his wing man, Major Carl Rodkins, as they flew in pursuit of the remnants of Japanese Admiral Ozawa's once powerful force of warships. At four o'clock on that fateful June afternoon just three days earlier, Captain Thompson along with 215 other American pilots had taken to the air for the 500 mile round trip that they hoped would secure their dominance in the Philippine Sea.

They were barely in the air when the message had come. Ozawa was 60 miles farther west than previously reported. After a few minutes of urgent trading of navigation information, Bruce heard Carl's comment. *No sense working this out both ways.* They would not have enough fuel to return to the aircraft carriers. The airwaves became strangely silent as the pilots flew on.

Two hours later, enemy ships were sighted and the quiet evening was shattered with explosions. As the American planes dropped their deadly cargo on the ships below, antiaircraft fire tore through the attacking planes. Bruce saw Carl take a direct hit. As his dying plane plunged toward the sea, Bruce had a vivid glimpse of Carl waving a bloody arm at him in farewell. There was no time to think. Not of Carl, of Karen, of anything but carrying out the mission. The months of vigorous training made his actions automatic. Through the deadly clouds of smoke, fire, and shells, Bruce flew on.

Nor did he know how many of them were left when they finally turned to return to the carriers. It was imperative that they maintain blackness and silence as they flew into the night, hoping to find their home ships. Using every trick he knew to preserve fuel, Bruce willed his aircraft to keep on flying. He forced Karen's face into the forefront of his consciousness.

"I'm coming home to you," he whispered.

A hoarse voice cut through the radio air silence.

"I've only got a couple of minutes gas left, Bruce. I'm bailing while I still have power. So long, Bruce. Tell Linda I love her."

Bruce grabbed his mike.

"Tom!"

But he could hear the descending whine of his friend's plane dropping toward the ocean below. He stared out the window, trying to spot the man's parachute, but all he could see was the glint of moonlight on the water below. His eyes fixed on the fuel gauge in front of him. By his calculations, the mother ship was at least fifteen minutes away. At most, he had three minutes of fuel left. Frantically, he began gathering his emergency gear. He pulled the plotting board from under the panel and did a quick calculation of his position. 15.1 North and 146 East.

Now the big decision. Ride the plane down and hope for a controlled crash that didn't kill him on impact or bail out with the parachute as Tom had just done. At least, he thought that was what Tom had done. He thought of his friend down in the cold seas below him. He reached over for the ejection button, but just as he did, the dark shape of something ahead of him seized his attention. The carrier? No, it was much bigger than that. Then a glimpse of moonlight outlined a sandy beach flanked with trees.

****

"Carolyn?" Adeline whispered in the darkness.

A pale faced framed in a sleeping bonnet appeared in the wagon opening.

"Adeline, is that you?"

"Kimberly's gone."

"What do you mean, gone?"

"She's disappeared. I think she's out in the woods with Marcus."

Carolyn pulled the cloth covering the opening aside and reached a hand down to help her friend.

"Here, come on up out of the cold. Marcus is up in the mountains with Mitchell and Alexander. I think you're imagining things, Adeline."

Adeline stiffened at that remark.

"I am not imagining anything. She's gone and she's been gone for two hours now."

"Oh my."

Carolyn pulled a blanket around her shoulders as she thought about the meaning of what Adeline had just told her.

"Would she have gone for a walk? Something could have happened to her."

"One does not go walking at midnight on a freezing night, Carolyn," Adeline told her.

"How can Marcus be with her and up in the mountains at the same time?"

"Do you really believe all that dot and dash stuff they do?"

"Well, I uh… don't you?"

"I care for Kimberly. I really do," Adeline said. "But she's changed. I don't know what's happened to her, but ever since last week, she's been strange. Almost as if she's been taken over by something. She's just not herself."

"What are you saying, Adeline? Are you implying that Kimberly has been... possessed?"

Adeline shuddered at the word. The two women stared at each other silently. Adeline waved her hand as if dismissing the idea.

"I don't believe in such things," Adeline said quietly. "But something's not quite right."

"She could be in danger," Carolyn said.

Adeline frowned. Carolyn was reprimanding her and she didn't like it.

"If she went out in the woods to walk, to relieve herself, or even as you suggest, to meet Marcus, that's not a safe place for a young woman to be alone." Carolyn thought for a minute and then said, "I'm going to wake the Simmons."

"Then I guess I'd better tell Emil," Adeline said.

****

The beach had proved way too short for a landing. The Hellcat F-6F slammed through the grove of trees, finally coming to rest deep within their protective cover. Despite his harness, Bruce was knocked unconscious by the violent impact. He awoke to find his feet wedged between a tree stump and what was left of the floor of the aircraft. Blood dripped down the side of his face from the imploding window that had covered him with glass shards.

Slowly, he unbuckled his harness and tried to assess the damage. He was alive, but a shooting pain through his right leg quickly told him that he hadn't escaped unscathed. He pulled his leg free, gritting his teeth at the fire that gripped his lower leg, and looked with dismay at his foot which hung at an odd angle. Before he even touched it, Bruce could feel the broken bones in his ankle and lower leg. Groaning, he eased himself out of the cockpit and onto the ground, standing on his left leg and clinging to the fuselage for support.

Looking at the damage his aircraft had sustained, Bruce's first thought was amazement that he was alive at all. His second was disappointment that the wreckage would not be visible from the air. Despite the swath of trees that the Hellcat had plowed through, the density of the trees was such that he doubted that even a glint of metal would show through the thick, interlaced branches with their broad waxy leaves.

He spent the first day getting oriented. A splint of branches and folded fronds gave little support to his leg. Even the slightest pressure on the bones sent shock waves of agony through him. He'd managed to hop from the water's edge to the cover of the trees and had looked around for something suitable to use as a crutch. He'd finally found a crooked tree branch but it was too short to be much more than a support. He'd hopped as far as he could in both directions, but the jarring motion made the sweat pour down his face. With his jaws clenched in pain, he'd finally settled on a location under a large coconut tree.

With the aid of a rock and his knife, he'd managed to pry some of the large nuts open. The sweet milk inside tasted good and he chewed on the dense white meat constantly to keep his mouth moist. His emergency pack contained a few days' rations, a small amount of water, and a condensation unit for collecting natural moisture. After he'd rested enough that the initial shock symptoms subsided, he struggled to his feet again and went in search of the battery for his aircraft radio. It had actually been thrown from the cockpit. He found it half buried in the sand. One terminal was broken off. Bruce tucked the battery under his arm and hopped slowly back to the plane. He placed the battery on the floor and then pulled himself in, moaning at the pain as he dragged his leg in behind him.

He inched into the pilot's seat and closed his eyes, allowing the waves of pain to subside enough so he could think. A new battery terminal. He scanned what was left of the interior. The front panel was still intact and his eyes focused on the screws along the edge. Using his knife, he removed one and screwed it into the broken terminal. The broken antenna wire lay on the ground and so once again, he eased his wounded body out of the fuselage. Restringing it took him nearly two hours. Ignoring his pain, he made his way back into the aircraft, hooked up the radio to the battery, and turned it on. He listened and transmitted for a full hour on Navy frequencies. Nothing. Either his band readings were inaccurate or the world had disappeared. Fearful of using up his battery, he turned it off and dragged himself back to his makeshift sleeping place beneath the coconut trees.

The next day, he watched the horizon constantly, ready to set off one of his emergency flares if he spotted something. But the ocean and skies were empty. By the end of the day, his hope of being rescued was replaced with a terrible loneliness. Once again, he tried the Navy frequencies. He heard static on one, but even that faded. Bruce buried his face in his arms. Suddenly, he pulled his head up and stared at the radio. He'd gotten his Amateur Radio license at age 12. Throughout this ordeal, the thought of his powerful transmitter back home in Seattle had flickered through his brain. He reached over and tuned the aircraft radio down to the 80 meter Amateur band. Due to the war, a radio blackout was in effect on the Amateur bands, but perhaps someone was listening.

While he had never tried using the military radio on those frequencies, it certainly had that capability. He settled on 3610 khz and grabbed the mike. By using the Push To Talk button as a code key, he could send Morse code, thus increasing the possibility of his being heard. The Beat Frequency Oscillator would allow him to hear a response.

Slowly, he sent his first message. SOS from W7DL. He sent the distress message over and over. Mindful of his battery, he limited his sessions to 20 minutes at a time. The ham bands seemed as dead as the military ones. Then on Day 3, a miracle happened. He heard a signal – one with strange echo-like qualities. *Hello anyone from KA7ITR.* Obviously, the operator was violating radio silence, but Bruce didn't care. He cried out with joy as he sent a response.

For an hour, he sat and listened in between his repeated transmissions. There was no further word from KA7ITR but just hearing him once was enough to give him hope.

97

Chapter 12

"W7DL from KA7SJP"

B ruce woke from a fitful nap and wiped the sweat from his face. Noon. Back home, Karen would be sound asleep. He wondered if she dreamed of him as much as he did of her. The vivid dreams were both torture and comfort. Waking to the bright sunshine, Bruce lay still, thinking. The most likely chance of his being rescued would have been in the first two days after the attack. By all odds, the fleet of carriers was probably well out of the area by now.

He reached over and grabbed his makeshift walking stick. It took all of his strength to get to his feet, and for a minute, the world swirled around him. He steadied himself and then made his way over to the aircraft. He'd set a schedule for himself. Transmit for ten minutes every four hours. It had been at this time yesterday that he'd had the brief contact with that Northwest station. Hopefully, that guy, whoever he was, might look for him again at the same time. He pulled his body into the pilot's seat and turned on the transmitter.

****

Emil grumbled mightily when Adeline woke him up and William Simmons was less than enthusiastic when Mary shook him awake too.

"Adeline, do you realize what a day's travel we have ahead of us in the morning? Don't you think a man needs his rest?"

"Kimberly has disappeared."

Grimly, the two men pulled on their boots and coats. They lit a torch of branches and set off into the woods. Adeline and Mary watched them go.

"Do you think they'll find her?" Mary asked.

"More likely, find *them*," Adeline said

****

Kim's feet and legs were totally numb beneath her. *Five more minutes*, she promised herself. Then she heard his signal.

KA7ITR or any station from W7DL, someone was sending over and over. The signal had the same eerie far away sound that Marc had described to her. She grabbed the code key. *W7DL from KA7SJP. What is your location?*

She flipped the HW-9 to receive and caught W7DL in the middle of another transmission. Apparently, he hadn't heard her.

I am an American Navy pilot down somewhere in the Mariana Islands. My location is close to 15.1 N Lat. And 146 E. Long. Please notify the Navy.

Kim's eyes blinked open wide. *Notify the Navy?* How could she tell him he was hearing a signal from 1845? She sat there motionless, totally blank as to what to say. Here she'd been hoping that she'd contact someone who could rescue them and here was a man who desperately needed them. Slowly, she took the code key.

W7DL from KA7SJP. My name is Kim and I am located somewhere in Oregon. My situation is somewhat unusual. I will try to help you, but you are the first person who has heard my signal. By the way, could you tell me the date?

She pressed the earphones close to her ears. Silence.

Kim pulled off her earphones. There was a light coming through the woods.

"Kimberly!"

It was Emil's low voice shouting for her.

"Oh no," Kim whispered as she hastily stuffed the HW-9 back into the bag. She started to yank the antenna line from the tree and then reconsidered. She pulled the makeshift telegraph from the bag and attached it to the line.

When the men entered the clearing, she pretended to be asleep, bent over the telegraph. Emil shook her shoulder.

Kim jumped and tried to stand up, but her feet were too numb to support her. William caught her before she fell.

"I uh, I uh," she stammered. "I wanted to talk to Marc but I haven't heard him."

The men looked at her suspiciously.

"You've been sending him messages from the camp. Why come out here?"

Kim shrugged, pretending to be embarrassed.

"I don't know. I guess we just wanted to have a private conversation."

"In the middle of the night?"

"It doesn't matter. I didn't hear him."

"It certainly does matter," Emil said sternly. "You've interrupted our rest. This nonsense has got to stop."

"Yes sir," Kim said meekly as she gathered up the telegraph gear and put it in the bag. She hoped neither of them would notice that the bag carried considerably more than the small telegraph.

They walked back to the camp in silence, the men leading the way. Kim longed to be able to talk to them, but she knew that anything she might say would be taken as just one more example of her improper behavior. A stony-faced Adeline peered out of the wagon as the three of them approached.

"Everything's all right," Emil told her.

Adeline looked at him questioningly but he was already on his way back to the tent area near the fire. With her head ducked down, Kim climbed into the wagon. Silently, she stowed her bag in the corner and sat down on the floor to take off her shoes.

"Well?" Adeline said demandingly in the dark.

"I'm sorry, Adeline. I didn't mean to concern you."

"Concern me? Just what were you doing out there in the middle of the night?"

Kim sighed.

"I was... trying to transmit a message."

"Landsakes, child, have you gone and lost your senses?"

"No, Adeline, I have not."

With that, Kim slipped in under the blankets and fell asleep.

****

Captain Bruce Thompson sat on the sand, staring out to sea. It was now 24 hours since he'd heard the signal from KA7ITR. Despite his repeated tries to contact him again, all he'd heard was static. But just now when he'd turned the radio on, there was another station – KA7SJP calling him. Again, the signal had the weirdest tone quality to it, but stranger than that was the operator's message. *"Somewhere in Oregon. By the way could you tell me the date."*

Bruce frowned. *Of all the ham radio operators in the world, I have to contact one who doesn't even know the date. Of all the rotten luck,* he thought. He rubbed his hand across his face as he sent back a reply. He had no idea how long his battery would last. He scooted into the shade out of the glare of the midday sun. His ankle was so swollen he felt as if he were dragging a melon attached to his leg. He waited until the throbbing quieted and then shaded his eyes and stared out at the horizon. He listened to his silent radio for another thirty minutes and then switched it off.

****

"Get up."

Adeline's stern voice broke through Kim's sleep. Adeline flung the cloth covering on the wagon open and yanked the blankets off Kim. Bobby stared at her curiously. He was fully dressed and stood on the ground juggling a couple of pine cones.

"We're leaving soon," Adeline said over her shoulder as she turned and marched toward the campfire where the tents were rapidly being taken down and stowed.

"She's really mad at you," Bobby said.

Kim shivered and pulled on her clothes.

"Yeah, I know."

"She's telling everyone how much trouble you are – how you ruined the night's sleep for Emil and the Simmons." Bobby wrinkled up his face and did his best at imitating Adeline's voice. "I wish I could send that girl back to Missouri."

"Great," Kim said.

Just then, Jasper Harrington ran by and Bobby, holding a stick across a pine cone like the wings of an airplane chased after him.

"Zoom, zoom," Bobby said as he skimmed his make-believe airplane along the ground.

Kim had forgotten to tell him that there weren't any airplanes in the 1800's. She wondered whether to try and stop him, but before she could open her mouth, he was out of sight around the corner of the wagon. She sighed and hurriedly put the inside of the wagon in order, smoothed her hair, and made sure the bag of ham radio equipment was hidden. She pulled a shawl around her and got out of the wagon. Hannah's husband, Jack, yelled to her across the clearing.

"Come over here. Hannah wants you."

Kim ran to their wagon, fearful that Hannah might have taken a turn for the worse. Instead, she was greeted by a smiling Jack who gave her a boost into their wagon. Inside, sitting up, looking almost radiant, was Hannah. Her hair was neatly brushed, she had on a fresh nightgown, and most important, she was nursing Baby Kimberly. The infant's loud sucking noises filled the wagon. Hannah smiled at Kim.

"I feel very healthy. Last night, I think my fever broke, and now this morning, I have milk."

"Oh Hannah, I'm so happy. You make sure you keep on taking those little pills, though."

"Until they're all gone, just like you said," Hannah reassured her.

Kim got down from the wagon.

"Move out, Move out, Move out," Emil was yelling to everyone as they hurried to hitch up their teams and break camp.

"Where's Mr. Fuller?" Kim asked Jack.

"In his wagon. He's gravely ill."

Jack looked at the somber expression on Kim's face. Hannah had told him about the magic pills, and he understood what that choice had cost their wagon leader. Silently, Jack walked around to the front of their wagon and straightened the yoke so he could lead the oxen into position.

By 8:00 a.m., they were underway. Adeline drove the team attached to their wagon since Emil had assumed the position at the front as leader. Kim and Bobby walked behind the wagon. Adeline had not spoken a word to Kim since waking her. At 10:00 as scheduled, Kim sent a telegraph message to Marc and received a reply. He and Mitchell and Alexander had shot a deer that morning. It was skinned and hanging from a tree right now. They would begin roasting the meat this afternoon so it would be ready for their arrival. *I miss you*, Marc sent.

Kim decided not to tell him about the "search party" that had brought her back to the wagons. That sort of thing was best told in person. Instead, she sent a message about Bruce and his plea for help. *What can we possibly do for him?* she asked Marc.

I don't know was his reply. *Let me think.*

"Adeline's watching you," Bobby said.

Kim looked up from the telegraph device in her hand to see Adeline glancing back over shoulder, shaking her head with disapproval.

"Let her look," Kim told Bobby. "I'm getting tired of this."

"Me too," Bobby said, kicking at the dirt. "The next time someone asks me why I talk about outer space, I'm going to tell them I'm an alien."

"With green fur and six hands?" Kim questioned as she reached over and tickled him.

"A gazillion hands and five gazillion feet." Bobby giggled. "And I'm going to tell them I have xray vision and can see their underwear just like Superman."

Adeline looked around again, almost as if their laughter annoyed her more than their science talk.

The group left the valley and began its way up the steep trail leading into the heart of the mountains. Kim watched her feet as they plodded through the dirt. She'd found that by counting off one hundred steps at a time, she could almost hypnotize herself into a rhythm that made the time go by. She knew that sometime soon, they would stop for a midday meal and a rest for the animals. After that, they would continue and soon she would be with Marc. How she longed to tell him everything that had happened.

They made their meal stop in a small clearing halfway up the mountain. Kim sat with the other women, drinking scalding tea and eating bread baked the day before. What was left of the meat was given to the men. Jack divided his portion with Hannah. May Belle Fuller didn't emerge from their wagon until the meal was almost over. When she did, she beckoned to Emil and William Simmons, two of her husband's closest friends. The group's conversation hushed.

They had all grown accustomed to the sound of Ben Fuller's coughing spells over the last few days. Now, the air was strangely silent. Adeline left her place by the fire and went to the wagon as did Mary Simmons. In a few minutes, Mary returned and spoke softly to Carolyn Malby. Kim was near them and turned her head slightly so she could hear what was being said.

"He's dying, Carolyn. May Belle's tried to rouse him, but he's in a death sleep. I think all that's left to come now is the rattle."

One by one, Mary went to the men and women and shared the sad news. She passed by Kim without so much as a look in her direction. Kim stood up and went back to the wagon where Bobby lay on the floor looking at the diagrams in one of Kim's science books. She climbed in beside him and sat on the floor cross-legged with her head in her hands.

"Are you sad, Kim?"

"Yes, Bobby; I'm sad."

"Me too."

Kim looked down at the small boy whose lower lip was quivering. In her concern for her own problems, she had pretty much ignored him the last couple of days. She reached over and put her arm around him.

"Bobby, when we get to Oregon, Marc and I are going to be married. And we want you to live with us."

"You do?"

Even though she'd never mentioned this possibility to Marc, she knew that he would willingly take in the orphaned boy.

"Yes, we do. Marc's going to need your help building a house, and I want to plant a garden. And when everyone gets settled, Marc and some of the men are going to build a school house and I'll be the teacher. You can be my helper."

"I'm not old enough to go to school."

"You're five now. When's your birthday?"

"February 1st."

"And then you'll be six. That's plenty old enough for school. Can I count on you to be my helper and wash the blackboards and stuff?"

"Okay," Bobby said.

The two of them looked up to see Jack standing near the end of the wagon.

"You'd both better come," he said.

"What is it?" Kim asked.

"Ben Fuller has passed on."

Chapter 13 -

"Rest in Peace, Benjamin"

There would be no more travel that day. The animals were tethered out and the men and women be - gan preparations for Benjamin Fuller's funeral. Kim sent Marc the news and he replied that he and Alexander and Mitchell would ride down to join them.

Another delay, Kim thought as she helped the women gather together their meager foodstuffs for the noonday meal. *And it's really my fault. If I had given the pills to Mr. Fuller, instead of Hannah, he would be alive and we'd be on our way.* She looked over at Jack and Hannah's wagon where the faint cry of Baby Kimberly floated into the air. How could anyone make that kind of decision? She saw the look on Jack's face as he joined the men in digging a grave and wondered if he were thinking similar thoughts.

The meal was nearly silent. May Belle didn't join them and Carolyn Malby carried a plate of food to her wagon. A half hour later, she carried it back untouched. Silently, Carolyn placed it beside the fire. Almost guiltily, a couple of the men picked it up and shared the contents. Nothing could be wasted.

Marc and the other men arrived on horseback around four. The group hastened to begin the burial lest darkness overtake them. Emil, now the leader of the wagon train by consensus, held his family Book of Prayer and read from it. The body of Benjamin Fuller, placed into a makeshift coffin made from two pine dressers, lay on the ground next to the open grave. Hold- ing Bobby's hand tightly, Kim stood at the edge, a respectful distance back from the older people who had been Benjamin's friends.

With his head bowed, Emil began the service.

"I am the resurrection and the life, saith the Lord; he that believeth in me though he were dead, yet shall he live: and whosoever liveth and believeth in me, shall never die."

Kim looked up and caught Marc's eyes staring at her across the group of people. May Belle Fuller leaned heavily on Adeline and Carolyn. All of the women formed a protective cloak of support around the grieving widow. Even Hannah, clinging to her husband's arm, joined the group. All of them were in this together. If God chose to take one of their members away, the rest of them would take care of each other.

Kim's thoughts and eyes blurred with tears. The words of Emil penetrated her consciousness as she thought of everyone dear she'd left at home – at both homes. If she, too, died on this trail, it might be months before her parents in Missouri ever found out. Her parents in Salem, Oregon would never know. A jerk from Bobby's hand brought her back to the present.

Marc and Jack and Mitchell were shoveling dirt into the grave. Emil's strong voice rang out over the sound of the dirt clods falling on the makeshift wooden box.

"Almighty God with whom do live the spirits of those who depart hence in the Lord, and with whom the souls of the faithful , after they are delivered from the burden of the flesh, are in joy and felicity; We give thee hearty thanks for the good examples of all those thy servants, who having finished their course in faith, do now rest from their labors..."

Kim concentrated on Emil's words. *Thy servants – finished their course – rest from their labors.* Is this what lay ahead for all of them? She didn't realize she was weeping until Marissa Harrington put her arm around her and led her away from the group.

"You must not cry in front of May Belle," she whispered sternly. "We must all be strong. Strength is what will get us through the mountains."

****

Captain Bruce Thompson struggled to his feet and hopped back to his airplane. It had been eighteen hours since he'd heard the young woman with the 7 call – the young woman who didn't know what day it was and who was violating radio silence. Painfully, he pulled himself up into the seat of the Hellcat and fired up the radio. As always, he checked the Navy frequencies first before moving to the 80 meter band. Silence on both. Not even a hint of the weird-sounding static he'd heard both times before making contact. Slowly, he climbed back down and sat on the sand. Time to assess.

He had enough emergency food rations to last a week if he supplemented with coconut. Water didn't seem to be a problem as it had already rained twice since he'd been here, and he'd managed to collect almost a quart the second time. He supposed eventually he might be able to rig some sort of fishing line and get food that way… and someday, someone would hear his signal. Even if the battery went dead before that happened, surely some ship or plane would spot him.

He imagined himself as a bearded, tanned island resident who would wave his rescuers in and offer them cracked coconut as a greeting. There was one slight problem with this scenario. His ankle, now swollen beyond anything Bruce could imagine, was developing red streaks up his leg. Whether it was the beginning of gangrene or blood poisoning, Bruce didn't know, but he knew that an infection of that magnitude without medical care would kill him. It was only a matter of time.

****

"We're moving out at daybreak," Marc told Kim as the two of them sat by the campfire that night.

"What's it like ahead?"

"Steep… but beautiful," Marc added, taking Kim's hand in his.

An ox lay asleep on the ground within earshot of the campfire. Even in slumber, its breathing sounded labored, as though no amount of rest in the world could restore its energy.

"Do you think we'll make it?" Kim asked.

Marc traced the outline of her hand against his own.

"I don't know. It certainly would have been easier a month ago."

The two of them stared silently into the fire. The flicker of candlelight from Adeline and Emil's wagon made shadows on the canvas. Adeline was probably busy writing in her diary. Kim wondered how she would record the sadness of the day.

"Are you going to try to contact the pilot tonight?" Kim asked Marc.

"I guess not. I think our midnight forays have attracted enough attention already. Maybe tomorrow if I can find some time alone. I wish I knew how to help him. He's absolutely the only signal I've heard on the bands."

"Why?"

Marc looked at her questioningly.

"Why any of this?" Kim repeated.

"I don't know."

****

At first light, the wagon train was on its way. The skies were thick with steel-gray clouds, but no snow or rain fell as they began their difficult ascent. What had taken Marc, Alexander, and Mitchell three hours to ride on horseback was an entire day's journey for the wagons. Kim tried to block the sound of the oxen's moaning breaths as they dug their feet in and valiantly pulled their cargo up the steep trail. Marc walked ahead as did the other men, giving their horses a much needed rest.

One, two, three, four, five, six, seven, eight, nine, ten, Kim counted off in her head as she watched her feet move ahead on the trail. How many times had she gone through that sequence? Perhaps that would be a good question for a math class. Not how many miles did the emigrants cover on the Oregon Trail, but how many footsteps?

****

"Kim?"

Kim looked up to see Bobby's dusty face beside him. Without being told, he had sensed that this was a day when he should walk. Her heart ached for his tired little body.

"Let's play a game," he suggested.

"Okay, what?"

"When my ship comes in."

Bobby was a whiz at memory games. Kim had learned that the first time she'd played a concentration game of cards with him. One by one, he'd uncovered the matching pairs.

"All right," she began. "When my ship comes in, it will have an apple on it."

Bobby knew the alphabet, but making sure words began with those letters was a little beyond him. So the list of the fictitious ship's cargo grew without structure which made it harder for Kim to memorize but didn't seem to bother Bobby. Marc pulled back from the head of the train just in time to hear Bobby deliver his winning turn. Kim recited the list, trying to remember a word.

"When my ship comes in," she said slowly; "it will have on it an apple, a spaceship, a cinnamon roll, five million hamburgers, eggs, Hans Solo, a giraffe, lots of French fries, ice cream, and... I'm stumped, Bobby."

"A television," he said triumphantly.

"That list makes me hungry," Marc said.

"Me too," Bobby agreed.

"Well when we get to the pine grove, there's a plump deer all skinned and cleaned hanging from a tree. We'll have that thing cooking in no time. Venison tonight."

"And venison stew tomorrow," Kim said, her mouth watering at the thought.

"What do you think about when you're walking along?" Marc asked her.

"Oh, lots of stuff, but sometimes I just count my footsteps."

"I design our house. I think I can see the whole plan in my mind."

"Tell me about it."

"Well, there's going to be a covered porch. And the front door will open right into the middle of the living room so that the first thing you see is a huge fireplace. We'll have a woodstove in the kitchen for cooking, but in the living room, I want a fireplace wide enough to put huge logs. Our bedroom will be upstairs. The heat will rise and we'll be nice and warm. I'm going to put in two other rooms upstairs," he said looking over at Kim. "One will be a nursery, and the other will be a sewing room for you."

"I don't suppose we could have indoor plumbing?"

"You bet. I've already thought of that. If I can figure out some way to rig an electrical pump, we'll have the water come right into the bathroom. And if not, I'll carry it for you."

"We'll be the envy of the neighbors," Kim said smiling.

"More like the inspiration. Once they see our flush toilet, everyone will want one," Marc said.

They visited like this for nearly an hour. Kim was grateful for the conversation. It not only took her mind off her aching feet, but it gave her things to think about for the future. When Marc left to join the men up front, she tried to continue those same thoughts. Bobby had finally succumbed to sleep and was napping in the wagon ahead of her.

Now they were high on the trail, looking down at a steep chasm beside them. The animals instinctively hugged the inward side of the trail. Every time they went around a bend, the men slowed them to a snail's pace as they maneuvered the wagons around the dangerous curves. Suddenly, there was a shout from up ahead. Kim squeezed past Adeline and Emil's wagon to see what was happening. The rear wheels of the Malby wagon had slipped over the edge and the wagon was in danger of plummeting down the embankment. The oxen, wild-eyed and gasping, clawed the ground, trying not to slip backward. Every man, woman, and child who could reach the wagon grabbed onto the wooden frame and pulled forward. For a few heart-stopping seconds, they lost ground, and it appeared as if the wagon and the animals would be lost.

As the wagon seesawed back and forth, Alexander Malby reached under the doubletree, trying to unfasten the animals' yokes. Marc, Grayson, and Nigel came running back from the front and added their effort to save the wagon. With a back-breaking wrench, the humans and animals struggled against gravity. Inch by inch, the wagon regained the trail.

The exhausted humans and oxen sank down on the ground. It took quite some time before the terror began to disappear from the animals' eyes, but finally, they lurched to their feet and began to pull the wagon up the trail again.

Jack, who had been one of the men who pulled the wagon to safety, had Hannah and baby Kimberly move to the front of their wagon. Hannah was in no condition to walk yet, but Jack wanted to make sure that if a similar calamity befell their wagon, that they would be where he could snatch them to safety. Kim had similar thoughts about Bobby who had managed to sleep through the whole event.

The clouds which had held their moisture all day opened up about 4 o'clock and a deluge of icy rain sluiced from the sky. Now in addition to the steepness of the trail, they had to deal with slippery mud. Just when Kim thought surely the animals couldn't make it any further, the trail leveled off and they entered the clearing Marc had described to her in his Morse code transmission.

The men set up arranging the wagons and setting the animals loose for the evening. An adequate covering of meadow grass would give them nourishment. Marc ran to get the deer. Kim heard his cry of anger from inside the wagon where she was helping Adeline get things ready for the evening.

"It's gone," he said as he and Alexander and Mitchell stared up at the tree branch where just a shred of the rope they'd tied the animal up with was left.

No one said anything. It was doubtful that this was the work of bears. Most probably, Indians, the same friendly tribe that had traded goods with them just two days before, had found the animal and taken it. It was no different than the steer their own group had slaughtered, Kim thought. Everyone was hungry and when food was found, it was finders keepers.

The men built a fire, but the steady rain kept it from ever really catching. They set up tents and crawled inside, and the women and children bedded down in the wagons. Kim pulled away the pile of soiled clothing in the corner and felt for the remaining candy bars left inside her sleeping bag. There were ten left. She peeled the paper from them and broke them into thirds and climbed out of the wagon.

"From my uncle," she said to William and Mary Simmons who took the offering suspiciously. "I was going to give them out last week, and I forgot."

She made her way from wagon to wagon; from tent to tent. All took the candy. When she had one piece left, she sought out Marc.

"I bet that's your last one," he said.

She held it out for him. With his eyes fixed on hers, Marc broke the chocolate in two and placed one half in her mouth. She took the other and raised it to his lips.

"The next time we do this will be with our wedding cake," he whispered.

Adeline's Diary

October 27, 1845

We buried Benjamin Fuller this morning. It troubles us all to leave our leader in a grave beside the trail, but we know his spirit goes with us. I'm very proud of my Emil for taking over the leadership of this group. In many ways, I think he should have been the leader all along. Of course, we will all miss Benjamin.

We are camped tonight in rain in a grove of pine trees. If the days ahead of us going through the mountains are anything like this one, then I fear that we may not make it. It has been a sorely troubling day for mind, body, and spirit.

No dinner tonight, but it does not seem to make any difference.

Chapter 14

A Game of Marbles

Adeline might have decided that food wasn't important, but Marc was awake before dawn.

"Where're you going?" Richard Faley, who shared his tent, asked him.

"Hunting."

"Just a minute; I'll go with you," Richard said, pulling on his boots.

The two men walked quietly through the dark campground. During the night, the rain had turned to snow and a two inch blanket of crystalline white covered the ground. Marc looked up at the moon. With the clear skies would come colder temperatures that could turn the top layer of snow to ice on the trail. Marc listened to his boots crunching through the snow as they made their way through the trees to a small mountain meadow on the other side.

The shot fired by Marc and then a second one by Richard woke Kim. She sat up so fast that she startled Bobby awake.

"What is it?" he whispered.

"Gunshots."

Kim looked over at Adeline but the woman was sound asleep, snoring softly. Bobby crawled to the wagon opening and looked out.

"Snow!" he said excitedly.

Kim sat beside him looking out at the beauty of the scene before them. Snow coated everything, casting a soft glowing light over the campground. But beyond the camp came the sound of the oxen and horses pawing through the white stuff trying to get at the grass. Kim struggled into her clothes. Quietly,

Bobby did the same and the two of them climbed from the wagon.

"Let's build up the fire," Kim told him, scooping up an armful of branches from under a pine tree.

They carried them to the fire and were rewarded with a cascade of sparks and crackles as they fed the smoldering logs with dry fuel. Kim tiptoed over to Marc's tent and peeked in. Somehow it didn't surprise her that he was gone. And it didn't surprise her either to see him and Richard a few minutes later coming in the camp, each carrying a dead wild turkey.

"Thanksgiving's a little early,"Marc said, grinning.

Kim ran to get the metal rods they used for skewering large roasts. She sat down on a tree stump and helped the men pluck and clean the birds. By the time they had them roasting, the rest of the people were waking up. Soon, a delicious aroma filled the campground. Kim stuck two large pans under the plump birds to catch the drippings. Nothing could be wasted.

****

Captain Bruce Thompson shaded his eyes to look out at sea. Was that a ship on the horizon or just another trick his brain was playing on him? In his mind, he had seen everything from Red Cross ships to hamburgers. None of it had been real. This did look like a vessel of some sort, though. He grabbed his binoculars. Yes! But instead of the familiar outline of a Navy aircraft carrier, this appeared to be a fishing boat of some kind.

He reached into his bag and grabbed one of his precious flares to load into the flare gun. He raised the binoculars to his eyes. Gone! For a half hour, Bruce watched the sea, willing the ship to come back. It didn't. Wearily, he wiped the sweat from his face.

Just relax, he told himself. *You have no idea who was on that ship. They might have killed you the minute they saw your American uniform.*

He looked down at his injured leg. *No,* he told his brain. *Don't say that.* But his brain formed the words anyway. *Perhaps it would have been better to just get it over with.* Just as quickly as that thought floated through his mind, a vivid image of Karen replaced it. He could almost hear her mouthing something. *Don't give up, Bruce. Don't give up.*

He grabbed a hanging tree frond and pulled himself up to a standing position. Using his makeshift crutch, he began the painful steps back to the airplane. The menacing teeth painted with warrior pride on the nose of the aircraft seemed to sneer at him as he forced himself up into the cockpit. Time to try the radio again. He hadn't heard anyone in two days, and he didn't expect to hear anyone now.

****

It was amazing what food did for the wagon train. If it hadn't been for the urging of Emil, Marc, and a couple of the other men, the entire group would have been content to sit under the trees, feasting on turkey all day. Thomas Amalind produced yet another bottle of whiskey, and in a rare show of generosity, offered to share it with the others. Emil told him to put it away and to prepare to move out.

By 10:00 o'clock, they were on their way.

Emil assigned James to ride ahead with Marc. Rosie, Marc's horse, had been limping badly for the last two days. Mitchell loaned him his bay mare and said he'd walk for the day. Kim tied Rosie to Emil and Adeline's wagon. Bobby sat in the back and spoke words of encouragement to the animal. However, when they reached a particularly treacherous section of the trail, Kim unfastened the horse, for fear the wagon might slip back and crush her.

Not only did the snow make the trail harder for the animals, but it also made it more dangerous. More than once, a wagon came precariously close to plummeting down into the canyon. Everyone breathed a collective sigh of relief when they reached a section where the dropoff wasn't so steep.

It started snowing again about noon and continued lightly, interspersed with periods of freezing rain, the rest of the day. Except for the two brief radio conversations she had with Marc, Kim kept her phony telegraph device attached to the solar charger on top of the tent, hoping for enough sun to re-charge the batteries. By noon, it was obvious there would be no charging today.

On and on they plodded. Kim's feet, numb from weariness, felt like icicles. The ache from the chill extended up her body, and she tried to think of anything other than how miserable she felt. She looked over at the other women, all walking except Hannah. Even May Belle had joined the group today, her face frozen with grief and determination. Making it to Oregon would be her tribute to her husband.

At 2 o'clock, Marc transmitted a message to Kim.

We have found a small clearing about two hours ahead of you. There is shelter, a good stream, and enough grass free of snow under the trees. We'll have a fire ready and hopefully some meat cooking when you get here.

Kim relayed that information to the others and it sustained the group as they struggled forward. All conversation ceased. The animals' labored breathing and the creaking of wagon wheels as they bounced over ruts in the trail were the only sounds cutting through the white afternoon. The sun broke through the clouds briefly just before they reached camp.

"I smell something cooking," Bobby said as they approached the flickering fire between the trees.

Like robots, the men arranged the wagons in the small clearing and turned the animals out to graze. No one even glanced at the fire where Marc and James were tending some kind of meat. Kim marveled at the women's self control. *Weren't they at least curious to see what dinner was?* Adeline dragged out their meager dinner supplies and began to set them up as she had every night for the 1700 miles.

Kim looked over at Marc who pointed at what was roasting on sticks. He shook his head with disappointment. Three jackrabbits – barely enough to feed six people, let alone thirty.

There were several loaves of stale bread left. Adeline began cutting them into chunks. They wouldn't use plates tonight. What was the point? After Emil offered thanks to God for "His gracious bounty," they lined up. Adeline handed each person a piece of bread and then Marc and James topped it with a small portion of roasted rabbit. Kim helped pour steaming mugs of watered-down coffee from a giant pot.

They ate quietly. The women retired to the wagons to ready them for bedtime. The men set up tents and then sat around the fire talking. The smaller children were already asleep. Bobby left Kim and Marc and wandered over to the Harrington wagon where Melanie, John, and Jasper were playing a game of marbles.

"Hi," Jasper said. "Want to play?"

Melanie helped him climb into the wagon, and he settled down on his heels to watch the game in progress. Their mother, Marissa, was over visiting with May Belle in her wagon. Jasper looked around to make sure she wasn't there and then whispered to Bobby.

"We've got a secret."

"Shhh, Jasper, you mustn't tell secrets," Melanie warned him.

"I've got a bigger secret than any old secret you could have," Bobby said.

John laughed.

"I do," protested Bobby, offended by the older boy's laughter.

"Like what?" Melanie asked.

"Something you wouldn't believe," Bobby said quietly.

"Bigger than a thousand dollars?" Jasper said.

"Jasper… you mustn't tell that," Melanie scolded.

"Lots bigger than that," Bobby said.

"Something big enough that you'd tell for my milk marble?"

Jasper stretched out his hand and opened the palm to reveal a pale blue marble with milky-white swirls through it. Bobby shook his head.

"Oh there you are," Kim said, poking her head in the wagon.

Bobby blushed red and scrambled to his feet. The other children watched him as he climbed out of the wagon.

"It's time for bed, young man," Kim said.

The Harringtons smiled at Kim but didn't say anything. Kim sensed that she had interrupted something and she hesitated as she looked at the marbles on the wagon floor.

"I used to play with marbles all the time," she said. "Until one day, this big bully at school just took them away. I never did get anymore. I guess I was afraid of losing them."

She reached over and picked up Jasper's "milk" marble.

"That's a really nice one," she said.

"I know," he replied looking over at Bobby.

Kim put it back on the floor.

"Well come on," she said to Bobby. "Adeline's about to have a cow."

The Harrington children watched Kim and Bobby walk across the campground. John Harrington turned to his brother and sister.

"Have a cow?" he said.

The others giggled.

****

Kim hoped Adeline would be bedded down by the time they got to the wagon, but the woman was hard at work on her journal. She looked up as Kim got into the wagon.

"You have two days of journaling to do," she said to Kim, handing her the slim leather volume.

Kim sighed. There was no use arguing with Adeline. She took the book and slipped into her quilts for warmth. Lying on one arm, she began to write in the dim light.

October 28, 1845.

Dear Diary:

I am not sure why I bother to put the date on these pages. What does a date mean anyway? Is time really accurate? Are we deceiving ourselves by believing that we are living a certain day? Days, hours, and minutes are not important. What matters is the care that individuals have for one another.

Kim paused. She was really getting in deep here.

Today has been a particularly hard one for all of us. The animals and humans are suffering from the cold and lack of food. And still, we go on because there is no other choice. I can only wonder what lies ahead.

She stopped. She was tempted to put "Hi Adeline" in big bold letters at the bottom of the page but decided against it. The woman was less than cordial to her these days and if they had to share sleeping quarters, there was no reason to make things worse than they were. Instead, she decided to compliment her.

I hope I can gain strength from the older members as they never seem to waver in their determination. Perhaps, someday, I will be an inspiration to others as well.

****

Captain Bruce Thompson fumbled in his pack for a pen and a pad of paper. He looked out through the shattered glass that used to be the window of his aircraft and leaned back in the seat, trying to take the pressure off of his throbbing leg. His hand shook as he began to write.

June 1944

My beloved Karen;

When I realized that I was no longer sure of the date, I knew I must write this letter to you. I know that my mind and my time on this earth are slipping away. If this aircraft is ever found, I hope someone will deliver this letter to you. Please, my darling, know how much I loved you and how hard I tried to keep my promise of coming back to you.

I've been thinking a lot of all the dreams we had. Remember how we talked of moving to a small town and opening a restaurant? I'm sure the Navy will give you a settlement for my death. If you still want to run a restaurant (and you're the one who's such a good cook), there's no reason why you couldn't realize that dream.

My father died when I was 8. You know that as I've told you the story of the logging accident many times. My mother never re-married. I'm not sure why because I remember several men who seemed eager to talk to her at church every Sunday. Somehow, I guess she thought she would be disloyal to his memory. My dearest Karen, I am giving you not only my permission, but also my wish that you find someone else to share your life with. I would not want you to be lonely as my mother was.

Someday I hope you will have children. You will be a perfect mother. I can see it in your face. The world will be a better place because of the children you have.

I guess that's about it. I have pain but I'm not suffering terribly. I find that I sleep more each day, and I suspect that one of these days, I just won't wake up when the infection in my leg gets bad enough. This is a beautiful island. The birds sing; the sunsets and sunrises are magnificent gifts from God. I spend my time imagining what it would be like to have you here with me – perhaps in a little hut that we built ourselves. Of course, we would be able to leave when we got tired of it.

The last two years of my life have been the best and that's because I've shared them with you. Know that my love will be with you always.

Your devoted Bruce.
XOXOXOXOX

Chapter 15

Hope and Courage

Karen Thompson looked out the window of the small apartment in downtown Seattle. She had just come home from her job as an elementary school reading aide and was putting some groceries away when she'd heard the knock on the door. She pulled the curtains aside that covered the living room window and peeked toward the door. Two men in Navy dress uniforms stood on the doorstep.

Karen felt her knees buckle as she hurried to the door. With her heart pounding so hard she could barely breathe, she pulled the door open.

"Mrs. Thompson?"

"Yes."

"May we come in?"

She stood aside weakly to let the men in. They seemed ill at ease. She knew what they were going to say before they did. The taller of the two cleared his throat.

"Mrs. Thompson, my name is Lieutenant Joe Kryser and this is Lieutenant Michael Hodges."

Karen stared at them. She felt her lips come together as though she were trying to speak but no words came out.

"May we sit down?"

In a trance, she moved toward the small sofa and two chairs that made up their living room furniture. The men sat on the chairs. Karen sank onto the sofa.

"Mrs. Thompson, it is our sad duty to inform you that your husband, Captain Bruce Thompson, is missing in action."

"Missing," Karen repeated softly, her voice barely audible. "Then he's not dead."

She didn't say it as a question, but as a statement.

"We don't know that, Mrs. Thompson. He was involved in a large operation near the Mariana Islands. Many of the aircraft ran out of fuel before they made it back to the aircraft carriers. The Navy managed to rescue most of the pilots. Your husband was never found."

Karen's eyes snapped open. Suddenly, she was the interrogator.

"Was his plane found?"

"No, Ma'am."

"And it wasn't shot down?"

"There's no record of that."

"Then he's alive,"she said simply, clasping her hands together against her chest. She turned to the men. "You are looking for him, aren't you?"

"There was a search in the area for several days afterward. He wasn't found."

"But you're still looking?"

"I'm not sure what the status of the search is," said Lieutenant Kryser.

"Well you'd better find out," Karen said, the color rising in her cheeks. "My husband is alive out there somewhere and he needs to be found."

The men stood up.

"The Navy will certainly keep you informed of any news," said Lieutenant Kryser.

Lieutenant Hodges handed Karen a white envelope which she didn't open. The men moved slowly toward the front door. Lieutenant Kryser turned to face her.

"We're terribly sorry to be the bearers of this news," he said. "Your husband will be in our prayers."

Karen didn't answer. She stood in the entryway as the men left, closing the door quietly behind them. For several minutes, she remained motionless, her hands clasping the white envelope. Finally, she looked down at it.

"No," she whispered. "No, this isn't correct. You'll come back to me Bruce. I know you will."

She walked across the small living room and opened a drawer in a small china cabinet. She slipped the envelope in and closed the drawer. Then she walked to the front window and stared out at the gray Seattle sky as tears ran down her cheeks.

****

It was Marc who woke everyone before sunrise. During the night, a low pressure system moved in from the west. The freezing level, had they been able to measure it, had been at 3000 feet the day before. Now, it was at 5000. Winds swept in moisture and just before daybreak, the rain began. Marc ran from wagon to wagon trying to get everyone moving. After little food and a tiresome day of travel, it was hard to get people to let go of the small comfort that their semi-warm bedding provided.

"It's not time yet, son," Emil told him.

"We have to be able to move at daybreak," Marc countered. "There's a big storm coming in. We need to move ahead and see if we can't find better pasture for the animals."

Emil didn't like being given advice any more than Adeline did, but he grudgingly got up and began harnessing the animals. There would be no breakfast this morning. By 7:00, they were underway. Marc came around to Emil and Adeline's wagon to check out Rosie who had spent the night standing on three legs. Marc bent to inspect her foot.

"The skin doesn't seem as hot as it did yesterday," Marc told Kim. "Come on girl," he said, coaxing the horse to take a step.

Reluctantly, the horse stepped forward. Marc wrapped her mane around his hand and for a brief moment buried his face against her neck.

"If she can't make the trail today, I'll have to..." his words trailed off.

"No you won't. She's going to get well. Rosie wants to make

it to Oregon just like we do," Kim said. She looked over at Marc who seemed lost in his own thoughts. "Marc?"

"What?"

"I was thinking maybe you should keep all the radio stuff in your wagon. Could you hide it in there?"

"Adeline snooping again?'

"I'm not sure, but I don't trust her."

Kim reached under some blankets in the corner and pulled out the packs holding their gear.

"I'll stow it. Don't worry; I don't think anyone's curious about my bedroll," Marc said.

"You're going to get better; aren't you girl?" Kim said, stroking Rosie's soft nose, after Marc left.

"The only thing that's going to be better about that horse is its flavor in the stew pot."

Kim whirled around to see Thomas Amalind standing half-drunk with a bottle of whiskey in his hand. Kim tried to ignore him, but he obviously wanted to tangle with her.

"You and your boyfriend with all your fancy learning. Think you're better than everybody, don't you? Well that horse will taste just the same dead as a dumb man's horse."

"Go away," Kim said, not making eye contact with the man.

"Nope! Didn't sleep very good last night count of my stomach growling. Think I'll take a little snooze in here."

He grabbed hold of the back of the wagon and hoisted himself. For a minute, it looked like the drunken man might fall off into the mud, but he managed to get a leg over. Kim heard a thump as he fell heavily onto the wooden floor of the wagon. She hesitated and then walked around front.

"Adeline?"

Adeline was on the ground helping Emil fuss with the yoke on one of the oxen. She looked up.

"Um, I don't know if you care or not, but Mr. Amalind is lying down in your wagon."

Emil and Adeline exchanged glances. *What was it about Thomas that made everyone afraid to cross him?* Kim wondered.

126

"Let him be," Emil muttered under his breath.

He swung into the saddle and shouted "Move out! Move out!" as he made his way along the row of wagons. He was wrapped in a rain slicker, one of the few in the group to have waterproof clothing.

Kim looked around for Bobby and saw him trudging through the mud from the direction of the Harrington wagon to join her. He started to climb up into the wagon, but Kim shook her head.

"Mr. Amalind is in there," she said.

"What's he doing in our wagon?"

"Well it's not really our wagon, Bobby. Remember that Emil and Adeline took us in because we didn't have a place to stay."

"My stuff's in there. He'll get it all stinky."

It was true. Thomas smelled like a brewery on bottling day. She had a brief vision of her wedding dress permeated with liquor smells. Thomas was already snoring, and Bobby giggled at the noise. Perhaps because she was so tired, Kim found herself laughing. Here they were, soaking wet, slogging along somewhere in the mountains 130 years before she was even supposedly born and there was a drunk man asleep next to her bridal gown. It was ridiculous.

Their laughter didn't last long. Once they were on the trail, the task of just putting their feet down on the trail became the overwhelming focus. The sound of the animals blowing and groaning, the creak of chains and wood, and the steady pelting of rain that stung their faces blocked out everything else. After two hours, Kim insisted that Bobby get up in the wagon.

"Take off those wet clothes and dry yourself on a blanket and then get in under my quilts."

"What about Mr. Amalind?"

"Don't pay any attention to him. You just lie down and take a nap."

On they went. In spite of the rain, they were actually making pretty good time. The rain melted the snow and the trail still had solid enough footing that they progressed fairly well.

By mid afternoon, the rain had slowed to a drizzle and Kim glanced anxiously at the sky, hoping for sunshine that would charge the batteries – the only radio gear that Marc left in her wagon as the solar charger was stretched out on top. The last transmission she'd had with Marc had been pretty scratchy. If they weren't able to charge the batteries soon, that would be the end of their telegraph demonstrations.

At three o'clock, she tried to reach him. He apparently wasn't able to read her transmission, but she copied his perfectly.

We're ahead of you about four miles. Tell everyone that we've found a meadow with good grass. The sun is even coming out and I've got the most incredible view of Mt. Hood. We're going to make it, Kim.

Kim felt her own spirits lifted by his optimism. She tried her best to convey that cheerfulness when she told the men his message. They listened to her but didn't reply. It was as though she were a small child whose opinions were discounted. It made her angry, but when she had resumed her place at the rear of the wagon, she noticed that the pace had been increased slightly.

They reached the camp an hour before dusk. It had been a long tiring day with no rest for humans or animals. The men turned the horses and oxen loose. They began grazing, gulping in the mouthfuls of grass that looked untouched. As soon as the Burchart wagon was positioned, Thomas appeared in the opening.

"Nice sleep," he said to Kim as he pushed past her to join the men.

Kim, cold, wet, and muddy, glared after him. Wearily, she climbed into the wagon and pulled her wet clothes off. She had one dry dress left. It wasn't clean, but it would have to do. She was still shivering when she joined the other women by the fire. A huge kettle bubbled noisily above the flames. Whatever was in it smelled delicious. Kim looked up at Marc who had come over to stand beside her.

"It's mountain grouse," he said. "We got a dozen of them," he said pointing at piles of roasted birds lying on a big tin pan to the side of the fire.

The women were dividing them up, allowing the men to take their fill first.

"So what's in the pot?"

"More grouse and some wild mushrooms I found."

"You're sure?"

"That they're mushrooms? Of course, I'm sure," Marc said, smiling at her.

Kim sank down onto a rock beside the fire. Suddenly, she was so weak she felt faint. In an instant, Marc was there handing her a cup of the stew. She ate it slowly, savoring the combination of flavors. For a long time after she was done eating, she sat motionless, feeling the hot food in her stomach.

"I think you need to go to bed," he told her.

"I told Bobby I'd read him a story."

"Don't you worry about him. He's over playing marbles with the Harrington kids. I just walked by their wagon."

Kim allowed herself to be walked back to the wagon. She didn't protest when Marc insisted that she climb in under the blankets. She had one brief thought that they did smell a bit boozy, but then she was fast asleep.

****

John Harrington sat cross-legged on the wagon floor. Fifty brightly-colored marbles were protected in the hollow made by his legs and he looked around smugly at the others.

"I'm not going to play with you anymore," Melanie protested. "You always win my favorite ones."

"I'd give you mine if I had one," Bobby said, and then turning to John, "I'll show you a neat trick if you give me a marble."

"Maybe," said John.

"Okay, put your two fingers up like this," Bobby said, pressing the tips of his forefingers together a few inches from his nose. "Now, look at them."

Melanie, Jasper, and John obediently followed his instructions and watched as Bobby brought his fingers closer to his eyes, looking quite cross-eyed as he did it.

"Keep your eyes on your fingers and they'll turn into sausages," Bobby said.

The kids did as he said and giggled as their fingers floated in front of them.

"All right," said John, rolling a red and white marble to Bobby. "You can have this one."

"I want the milk marble," Melanie pouted. "Do another trick, Bobby and win it for me."

"There's only one way you can get that one," said John.

"How?" Bobby asked.

"You know."

"Will you tell me your secret too?"

John looked at Jasper who shook his head "no" but Melanie blurted it out.

"If you tell us yours."

"I don't know," Bobby hesitated. "I'm not supposed to."

"Oh, it's probably a stupid secret anyway," Jasper said.

"Yeah not like ours that our father has a thousand dollars." Melanie clapped her hand over her mouth in horror at what she'd just said.

"We don't know how he got it," said Jasper, "but he's got it hidden under the wagon seat, and he thinks he'll have a headstart on everyone once we get there."

"Oh," said Bobby, not interested.

"So what's yours?" John said as he rolled the milk marble around in his hand.

Bobby stared at the marble and took a deep breath.

"Me and Marc and Kim were sent here by electricity."

"By what?"

"Electricity. You know the stuff that makes those dit dah things work."

"Sure you were. Sent from where?"

"From Oregon. Where we live, there're cars and planes and telephones and televisions and things like that. Last week, I turned on the Spark Gap."

The children stared at him as he started to cry.

"I didn't mean to," Bobby sobbed. "I wanted to help."

Melanie shook her head.

"What's a Spark Gap?" Jason asked.

"A radio thing that people used a long time ago," Bobby said, sniffling.

"What's radio?"

"You know… what you listen to music and news on."

"Yeah, and the moon is made of green cheese," John said.

"No, it's rocks and white stuff."

"Huh?"

"The astronauts have brought some of it back to earth. I've seen it at the museum."

John burst out laughing.

"You're crazy," Jasper said.

"I am not and you promised to give me that marble."

"Oh, take the dumb thing. Playing marbles is for little kids anyway," John said as he plopped the milk marble into Bobby's hand.

Adeline's Diary

October 28, 1845

Dear Diary:

I am in a much better mood tonight than last Even though today was just as cold, if not colder, we all seemed to tolerate the adversity better. I believe that is because we covered a great deal of ground — perhaps 18 miles. I was always brought up to believe that inaction is the source of much unhappiness and I know that it is true. As long as we are able to move forward, to do something productive toward reaching our destination, then our spirits stay alive. I will remember the feelings of today the next time someone suggests we rest.

Unfortunately, Thomas chose to ride in our wagon all day. That is not to my liking, but as we all know, he is the one who has a great deal of the money that made this journey possible. There isn't a day that he doesn't hold that fact over all of us. It makes me ill to think of how hard many of our good men have worked for very little and then Thomas inherited all that money from his father's shipping business when he died. Fortune does not shine equally on all.

Chapter 16

Tragedy on the Trail

Jasper told Bobby he thought he was crazy for his saying he had come from the time of television and moon walks. Bobby not only insisted that it was true but drew a sketch of his five year old impression of a space shuttle. When he asked for another piece of paper, John found an old newspaper folded in a trunk and Bobby made a couple of paper airplanes for them in a jet-like design Marc had shown him. He couldn't get either one to fly, but the Harrington kids looked at them in amazement and saved them after Bobby went back to his wagon.

Later, when their parents came to bed, Melanie blurted it all out, and after a little prodding, Jasper produced the space shuttle drawing and the paper planes. Marissa and Nigel Harrington examined them carefully and listened as Jasper related some of Bobby's words.

"If you ask me, he's a bit touched in the head," said Marissa. "In fact, I think all three of them – Marcus, Kimberly, and Robert have acted very strangely this past week."

Nigel sat quietly, mulling over the conversation.

"Did he say when this happened?" he finally asked.

"Last week," Melanie said.

"Well something happened to them last week," Marissa said. "But I think it was that sulfur water they drank from that bad spring. They've all been different ever since."

"It does seem odd that Marcus waited until last week to invent his telegraph machine. We could have certainly used it earlier in the trip," Nigel reflected.

"Maybe he just thought of it," John said.

"I don't know. I think I'll have a word with some of the others about this," Nigel said.

Within an hour, everyone in the wagon train knew about Bobby's strange revelations. Most of the men passed it off as the imagination of a five year old, but several of the men indicated that indeed "this was something to think about," and that the trio bore close watching.

Hannah's husband, Jack, fiercely loyal to Kim ever since she saved Hannah's life, was the one who told Marc what had happened.

"Oh no," groaned Marc. "Just what we need. More suspicion. If anything, these people need to trust me more, not less, in the days ahead."

"So is it true?" Jack asked.

"What?"

"The things Bobby said about you being from another time."

Marc put his hands on his hips and smiled at Jack.

"Now what do you think?"

"I think perhaps that young Robert does not have enough to occupy his mind," Jack said.

"Right," agreed Marc.

And that was the way it was left. But the next morning as they prepared to move out in a driving rain, Marc and Kim could feel the eyes of the others watching every move they made.

Marc came around to the back of Emil and Adeline's wagon for a few minutes of whispered conversation with Kim before they began the trek for the day.

"Hey, she looks better," Marc said examining Rosie.

"That's because Thomas threatened her with becoming stew," Kim said.

"And stew she'll be," chuckled Thomas behind them.

He grinned maliciously at Kim and Marc as he climbed into the wagon for another day of napping. Marc took Kim by the arm and pulled her away out of earshot.

"That's terrible that the people allow him to do that. Emil's oxen are about ready to give out, and that man gets a free ride."

"I know," Kim said.

"When we get to Oregon, I don't want anything to do with him."

"When we get to Oregon..." Kim repeated softly.

"We will," Marc promised her.

"Have we got enough battery power left to talk to each other today?"

"I hope so," Marc told her. "But the 12 volt on the HW-9 is definitely dead. I tried it last night."

"You did? You risked having someone see you? I'm not sure that was a good idea."

"That pilot needs us... and besides I went quite a ways in the woods."

"You must be exhausted," Kim said. "Do you ever sleep?"

"When we get to Oregon, we're going to sleep for a week," Marc said.

Kim smiled and reached up to touch his gaunt, bearded cheek. Marc bent to kiss her and then hurried off to join the men at the front of the wagon train. He and James were going to ride ahead today. Emil had suggested the change and Marc suspected it was because he trusted James more than Mitchell who was younger and a friend of Marc's.

****

Captain Bruce Thompson's radio battery wasn't dead yet, but every time he flicked the "on" switch, he held his breath until he saw the lights glow, indicating it was still working. It didn't seem logical that a functioning radio wouldn't pick up anyone, but the airwaves were totally silent.

He started writing down the time and what he thought was the date of each attempted transmission. In between his four hour schedules, his mind wandered in and out of lucidity. He didn't fight it anymore as he had at first. When he was dozing on the beach and dreaming of Karen were the only really bearable hours of the day... and night.

When he had entered college, the freshman English exam had consisted of the following question: "If you were stranded on a desert island, what three books would you take with you?" The topic lended itself nicely to three paragraph development with topic sentences and supporting details. Bruce remembered that he'd chosen the Bible – lots of good stories; the dictionary – lots of good words; and a history of inventions. He wrote that he would use his time analyzing the great inventions of the world and come up with a few of his own so that when he came back, he could become a millionaire. He got a 95 on the essay and was placed in the accelerated freshman English.

"When he came back." How easily, he had written those words. But then how easily, he had taken everything in his life. Even though it had been difficult growing up without a father, Bruce had always had an optimistic view of life. Get a good education, find a good wife, be honest with others, and what could go wrong? Then the war came along. But even up until last week, that hadn't seemed a major detour. He loved the flying, loved the camaraderie of the men, and he loved serving his country.

Would he have done anything differently? Probably not. This was just the luck of the draw, and he'd drawn the short stick. He groaned as he tried to move his leg out of the afternoon sun that was creeping in under the trees and thought of the men in his squadron. How many of them had died at sea? Were there any who were stranded on islands like he was? For all he knew, there could be someone on the other side of this one, but without being able to walk, there was no way he'd ever know.

****

By noon, the wagon train had moved five miles. Not too bad for a stormy day. If the snow held off and they made it through the higher elevations in the next few days, they'd be on the downhill side going toward the Columbia River.

They stopped for an hour at one and ate the rest of the stew from the night before. Many of the oxen simply sank to the ground, too exhausted to graze during the meal stop. Kim could no longer bear to look in their eyes. They were hungry, exhausted to the point of collapse, and yet they willingly took up their burden, simply because man asked it.

If we make it, I'm going to make sure you all have the finest hay and grain to eat every day, she mentally promised them. Once again, the image of Marc plowing their own garden with a plow pulled by well-fed contented oxen flashed through her mind. She would be standing on the back porch, shading her eyes with her hand, watching him finish the planting and waiting for him to come in and taste the freshly-baked apple pie cooling on the kitchen table.

She came out of her daydreams to hear Bobby sniffling beside her. He was plodding along, staring at the ground.

"What's the matter?" she asked him.

"The Harringtons won't let me walk with them."

"They won't?"

"No, Jason said his father said they can't even talk to me anymore."

Kim put her arm around him and attempted to wipe his tears, but the rain coursing down both their faces made any try at drying anything futile.

"They just don't understand," she said.

"I'm sorry. I told the secret," he said.

"Don't worry about it. I think you did a good job keeping that secret as long as you did."

"You do?"

"Yes, I do, and Marc does too. Just forget about those folks and think about that treehouse we're going to build for you once we reach Oregon."

"Maybe Jason would like to come play in it," Bobby said.

"You know something? I just bet he might," Kim said.

On and on they walked. When the trail was especially slippery, they went single file and a man held on to the yoke of each pair of oxen, encouraging them to find their footing. The rain was relentless and the wind whipping it in their faces made it truly painful like a thousand needles being thrown at them again and again. Kim bowed her head and watched her wet feet slosh through the mud. Bobby reached the limit of his five year old endurance and she insisted that he ride in the wagon.

He couldn't sleep though due to Thomas's snoring so he sat up next to the back of the wagon, reaching out to give Rosie an occasional pat. They were first in the line of wagons today, and Kim could feel the eyes of Carolyn Malby boring into her back. Behind her were the Simmons, then the Harringtons, the Hodges, the Dearborns, Hannah and Jack Worth, May Belle Fuller, and then the wagon belonging to the single men.

That was the wagon where Thomas Amalind was supposed to be, but since he'd decided that sleeping all day in the lead wagon was more to his liking, that was where he was. Once again, Kim felt her spine bristle with resentment at the advantage this man was taking of the others.

They were going up an incline now. The trail curved up the side of the mountain with huge stands of fir trees both above and below them. The oxen instinctively hugged the right side of the trail to be as far away from the cliff as possible. But for the last hour, small rocks and mini mud slides, caused by the increasingly heavy rain, forced them to walk very near the edge.

Suddenly, Kim felt a chill of premonition sweep over her. She looked up at Bobby sitting almost on the wagon edge now and then with a shudder glanced out of the corner of her eye at the chasm below them to the left.

"Hey Bobby."

"What?"

"I've got an idea."

"A game?"

"Well not exactly. See how Rosie's not limping very much?"

"Yeah."

"Well supposing you ride her for awhile. That way we can see if she's able to carry someone."

"I don't want to hurt her."

"I don't think you will. Just for a little while anyway."

Kim reached forward and untied the patient horse who responded with a soft whinny. She knew better than to do anything that slowed the momentum of the wagons so she beckoned to Bobby to climb down from the wagon. He did and jumped to the ground, splashing mud up his already filthy pants.

"Okay, come around here to her left. You know how cowboys in the movies sometimes run and jump on a horse?"

"Yeah."

"Well, I'm going to lift you up on her while you're walking and you have to hold her reins, okay?"

"Okay."

Kim looped the reins over Rosie's head and tied them together in a knot, letting them lie on her neck. The horse was so well-trained, she would follow the wagon even without a bridle. Kim picked up Bobby and plopped him on the horse's wet, bare back. Bobby grinned as he leaned forward and picked up the reins.

"You can hold onto her mane too if you feel like you're slipping."

"Okay."

Just as the words left his mouth, Rosie neighed and half-reared. Panicked, Kim caught her bridle, but Bobby was already deposited on the ground. There was a huge roar and crashing noise as a ton of mud swept down the hillside from above, slamming into the wagon, and tossing it over the cliff like a toothpick. Kim watched in horror, clinging to Rosie's bridle. The wall of mud crossed her feet pushing her backwards. Her hand slipped loose from the leather reins as she became part of the mud oozing over the edge.

"Kim!"

It was Bobby clinging to her arm, pulling desperately to keep her from going over the precipice. Soon another hand was on her arm and Kim looked up dazed to see Carolyn Malby dragging her to safety. A piercing cry cut through the rain.

"Adeline!"

Kim sat on the ground with a quivering Bobby next to her. The mudslide was at least eight feet high. It had come within inches of sweeping her away, and with a shaking realization, she remembered taking Bobby down from the wagon just seconds before.

"Adeline!"

Emil's anguished cry rang out again, and Kim forced herself to look over the edge where their wagon lay at the bottom, buried under tons of mud. In it were Adeline and Thomas.

Calling out for others to help, Carolyn and Alexander Malby were halfway up the mudslide, clawing with hands and feet to gain on the mountain of mud. Carolyn screamed as the earth slipped some more, but her husband gave her a shove that sent her over the top and he soon followed.

"We need help over here!" he yelled.

William Simmons and Grayson Hodges, using the fast-filling toe holds made by the Malbys, scrambled up over the mud. Amidst nervous whinnying from the horses and the clatter of wood and steel as men and women forced the animals to back up the wagons away from the slide, Kim pulled herself to her feet. Holding Bobby's hand tightly, she walked over to the trembling Rosie and picked up the reins.

Chapter 17

Assessing the Damage

The animals were used to moving forward, not back ward, so it was with great difficulty that they were backed a quarter of a mile down the trail to an area large enough where they were no longer in danger from the unstable ground. Kim and Bobby led Rosie and tied her to a tree. When Kim was sure that Bobby was safe under the care of Hannah, she ran back to the slide area. Someone had thrown a rope over it, and Kim ascended the slippery mass.

Her feet sank into the cold mud, and it took all her strength to pull each one out. Suddenly, all the shock and fear at what had just happened turned to anger and with energy she didn't know she had, she forced her body up and over the top. For a few seconds, she paused on top of the mud, just gasping at the scene below.

Mitchell, Marc, James, Alexander, Emil, and Nigel were dig ging frantically at a mud-covered body. Kim couldn't see who it was as they were all kneeling, scooping the mud away with their bare hands. Then she heard a groan.

"Ohhhh."

Could it be? James moved over a few inches and Kim caught a glimpse of the mud-coated face of ... Adeline. Quickly, Kim slid down the other side of the mud, landing with a plop at the bottom. None of the men looked up. They were all too busy extricating the woman.

"I've got her right leg," Marc said.

"Here's the other," said James.

"Careful now," Emil cautioned as they gingerly lifted Adeline and carried her to the shelter of some trees hanging over the trail. Marc looked up as Kim ran to the group.

"Are you okay?" he asked, seeing Kim's mud-coated legs.

"Ohhhh," groaned Adeline.

"Yes and Bobby, too," Kim said quickly as she took off her shawl and knelt beside Adeline. "And so is Rosie," she added, gently wiping the mud from Adeline's eyes and nose.

Adeline groaned again and her eyes flickered. Emil looked on as Kim and Marc ran their hands over Adeline's extremities.

"I think her right leg is broken," Marc said. "I can feel it right below her knee."

"Biggest problem right now is going to be shock," Kim said. "We've got to get some blankets."

Without a word, Mitchell ran toward the mud slide and began climbing it. Within minutes he and Richard Faley were back with an armload of quilts. Kim and Marc shoved some of them under Adeline to make a barrier between her and the cold ground and they piled the rest on top of her.

"That mud on her skin may be insulation," Kim said. "Let's not clean it off just yet."

Adeline was shivering and muttering. Emil crouched beside her, reaching out helplessly to pat her head.

"Don't leave me, Adeline," he whispered.

Marc shoved some branches under legs and Adeline groaned from the pain.

"Why are you doing that?" Emil asked angrily. "Can't you see she has enough pain?"

"She's in shock," Marc told him gently. "We need to get the blood flow down to her heart and brain so she won't pass out on us."

Emil shook his head. Obviously, this was just another strange idea from the young man.

****

Karen Thompson ran to answer the ringing telephone.

"Hello," she answered eagerly.

"Mrs. Thompson, this is Major Carl Rodkin. I was in your husband's squadron."

Karen could feel her heart beating in her throat.

"Yes?"

"I'm calling from the Navy Hospital in San Francisco. I just wanted to tell you that I was flying next to your husband when I went in."

"You saw him?"

"No, just before I was shot down, he said he was almost out of fuel. We were still fifteen minutes away from the ship then. I'm not sure if he ejected or landed it in the ocean."

"The officers who came just said that he was missing in action, but they seemed to imply he was dead," Karen said, tears forming in her eyes.

"Yes, I'm sure that was the opinion of everyone when he didn't show up in the search, but..."

"What?" Karen asked.

"I probably shouldn't be raising false hopes because I don't have any basis for them, but I've just got this really strong feeling that he's alive."

"After all this time? How could he be?"

"There're a lot of islands."

"Well why aren't they searching them?"

"I'm sure there've been some flyovers, but there's also enemy action in that area."

"But if he's still alive..."

"I do apologize for calling you. It's just that... well, I had a dream about him the other night. That's where he was. On an island. If I were able, I'd lead a search party myself "

"Are you wounded?"

"Yes..." The major hesitated and then quietly said. "I lost a leg."

"Ohhh. I'm sorry."

Karen held the phone glued to her ear while she wished Major Rodkin well and asked him to call her again. When she hung up, she went to the front window and stared out at the sky for a long time.

****

After Adeline was stabilized and the wagons and animals secured, the men attacked the mud barrier with shovels. Scoop after scoop of mud, they threw over the trail edge, but instead of getting smaller, the unstable barrier was getting larger. Because of the overhang, it wasn't possible to see the slope above where the slide had originated. Emil called the work to a halt and took several men with him some distance back down the trail near the wagons. From there, they climbed the hillside and went laterally until they had a good view of the top of the slide area.

"It's hopeless," Marc told Kim after they came back down. "There are several uprooted trees and the whole surface is coming down. The more we remove, the more dirt will slide. Eventually those trees will be with it. We're really lucky our whole group wasn't pushed over."

Adeline couldn't be moved, and since each trip over the top of the slide was increasingly hazardous, Emil waited with his wife, while the rest gathered back at the wagons to decide what to do. Some of the women had put together a lunch of sorts – coffee, stale bread, and a small pot of beans which yielded less than a half cup for each person.

"I think we should go back to the Grand Ronde Valley and wait until spring," said James Dearborn.

"We'll starve," said Jack, quietly, putting his arm around Hannah and the sleeping baby Kimberly.

"No we won't," countered Mary Simmons. "Surely there'll be some traders who come through and we can buy some things from the Indians."

"Enough to feed us all?" Grayson Hodges asked.

"I'd like to scout some of the side trails. See if there's another way," said Marc.

"There are no other ways," said James Dearborn. "If there were, they'd be on our maps."

Marc clenched his fists. This was the problem with this group. They only believed in what had already been discovered.

"I'm going to go anyway," he said, standing up. "Anyone want to go with me?"

Mitchell rose to his feet. Marc turned to Kim.

"I'll contact you in three hours."

The afternoon passed with tedious work. The rain finally stopped, allowing them to build several small fires. People changed into what dry clothing they had and hung their mud-soaked garments near the flames to dry. Inch by inch, the men went over the animal harnesses, the wagon wheels, and any other parts they thought might have suffered damage. No one mentioned Thomas Amalind, but the expressions on faces as they caught a glimpse of the wreckage down below showed that his fate was on everyone's mind.

On a hunch, Kim walked back to the wagon that had belonged to Bobby's parents until their death. May Belle Fuller was standing nearby talking to Carolyn Malby.

"Will you two ladies watch what I'm about to do?" Kim asked. "I don't want anyone accusing me of stealing."

They seemed surprised by the tone of her request, but the two of them obligingly followed Kim as she crawled into the wagon. In a corner, a small cloth satchel belonging to Thomas sat under some dirty quilts.

"You think that belonged to Thomas?" Kim asked.

"I reckon so," said Carolyn.

"Yes, I saw him carry that into the wagon the day we left," May Belle said.

Kim knelt beside the bag and opened it. There had been so much talk of his riches and how he planned to help finance their entire community once they got to the Willamette Valley, she almost expected gold to come rolling out. All she found were dirty clothing items, two bottles of whiskey, and five potatoes. The women seemed as surprised as Kim.

"Well I do wonder," said Carolyn. "Where is all the money he talked about?"

"I'd like to make these potatoes into soup for Adeline and the two nursing mothers," Kim said.

The women nodded absently, but it was clear their thoughts were on what was not in Thomas's bag rather than what was.

Kim hunted for a little wild parsley and the last of the mushrooms Marc had gathered. She simmered them with the chopped potatoes over the flames and when it was done, she carried a sealed container with a handle on it to the landslide. She tied the handle to the rope.

"Emil?" she called.

"Yes."

"Pull the rope over."

She watched the tin container bounce along the muddy surface and prayed the lid would stay on. In a few minutes, Emil threw the rope back. It was just out of her reach, but if anyone else decided to go over the slide, it would be there as a handhold.

Three hours later, she turned on her make-believe telegraph to listen for Marc. There was static and she could hear some intermittent beeps, but the signal was too broken up to get solid copy. She made out one phrase – *a way, but very hard.* She sent a message back not knowing if he would receive it. Their remaining batteries were dead and their only hope of charging them lay at the bottom of the canyon under mud along with her wedding dress and Thomas.

Chapter 18

A Difficult Decision

There was really nothing to eat. The travelers gathered around the fire and held mugs of hot water in their hands, sipping it slowly. It was dusk and Kim anxiously watched the trail where Marc and Mitchell had gone.

"I think he said there was a way," she told some of the people, but they seemed too dazed to hear her.

The wind had picked up again, probably the forerunner of another storm, and its cold tentacles flicked the canvas of the wagons and forced the animals to huddle together for warmth. Kim looked at her filthy dress flapping from a tree branch. She was wearing one of Hannah's dresses until her own dried, and although Hannah had told her to keep it, she planned on putting her own back on.

She turned her head as Rosie whinnied at Marc and Mitchell approaching. The two men quickly unsaddled their horses and walked over to join the others at the fire. She expected Marc to blurt out any news he had, but he motioned for everyone to gather around the fire.

"We have a very difficult decision to make," he said slowly. "There is another trail that goes around this mountain, but it's narrow. We can make it through single file, but the wagons can't go."

He paused, looking around at each person in the group.

"After we reach the other side of this mountain, it flattens out for as far as we could see," Mitchell offered helpfully.

"I say we go back to Grand Ronde," William Simmons said. "Without Thomas, we have no money to start our farms anyway."

Kim couldn't stand the mystery any longer. Even though she knew that every time she spoke out, she further destroyed her "ladylike" behavior, she couldn't help it.

"How much money was Mr. Amalind promising you?"

"A thousand dollars for each of us," said Mary Simmons. "He said he had inherited his father's fortune and he wanted to move to Oregon and start a community."

"Did you ever see that money?" asked Marc.

"No, he was going to have it sent from New York once we arrived," said May Belle Fuller.

"We didn't have a lot of time for questioning," Carolyn Malby said defensively. "Thomas came into town just as we were trying to get a group together to go to Oregon. We told him we weren't sure we could go because we had very little money among us, and he told us..."

"Money was no problem?" Marc finished the sentence for her.

"Well, yes, I guess that was the way he put it," Alexander Malby said.

"Did it ever strike you as odd that a man who is basically a drunkard could hold onto that much wealth?"

"Guess we didn't think much about it," said Alexander.

"We all just wanted to go to Oregon so badly," said May Belle Fuller. "Thomas presented himself as the means to do it."

"He must have wanted to go to Oregon, too," said Marc softly. "And you gave him a free ride. I imagine that once you got there, you would have never seen him again."

The people stood quietly. The image of Thomas lying in wagons all day drinking and eating more than his share of the food every night was vivid in their minds.

"We have no food, we have no money, and if we leave the wagons behind, we'll have no supplies," said James Dearborn, his voice thick with emotion.

Mary Simmons began crying. For a few minutes, no one spoke. Mary's sobs and the crackling of the fire filled the air as they stood, grim-faced. With an exasperated sigh, May Belle Fuller turned to Mary.

"Oh stop your sniveling, Mary. There's lots of us that have more to cry about than you do."

Mary's mouth fell open in surprise, but her tears stopped.

"We'll never get anywhere if we stand here feeling sorry for ourselves," said May Belle.

Kim looked at the widow of the wagon train leader with admiration. This was the kind of strength that would get them there.

"Exactly how wide is the other trail?" asked Grayson Hodges.

"About six feet," said Marc. "Narrower in some places."

"Supposing we made some carts," said Grayson.

The others looked at him, trying to imagine what he was suggesting.

"If we broke down the wagons, could we make carts with the wheels closer together?" Grayson asked.

"Maybe wheelbarrows," said Mitchell. "There's a strip about twenty feet long where's it barely three or four feet."

"All our things," sobbed Mary, starting to cry again.

"Oh be quiet, Mary," commanded May Belle.

"I think we need to go back to the valley and wait," said William Simmons. "How many in favor of that?"

"No," said Grayson, looking over at his wife holding their sleeping baby. "We're going on."

From a wagon came the soft whimpering of Jack and Hannah's baby. Kim watched the people's faces as they weighed the consequences of the decision they were about to make.

"I have something to say," said Nigel Harrington, clearing his throat. "I know all of you were depending on Thomas Amalind's money to get you started. I've never mentioned this because I thought everyone would be taken care of, but now it seems as if we all have to pool whatever we have. We have money," he said looking over at Marissa who nodded her head slightly.

"Marissa's father died last year and he left our children one thousand dollars for their future." Nigel paused as the group listened intently. "All of you are our children's future. When we reach Oregon, we're counting on each of you to help us just as we will help you. None of us can do this alone. I don't know how far that thousand dollars will go, but as far as Marissa and I are concerned, it belongs to all of us. Now let's get busy building those carts."

"Amen," whispered May Belle.

Marc put his arm around Kim and held her close.

****

There was no sleep that night. The women heaped wood on the fires, and the men pulled out saws and began to work on the wagons. All of the children, including the two babies were bedded down in one wagon under the watchful eyes of Susan and Hannah.

It was decided that each family would have one wheelbarrow. A wagon had four wheels, so one wagon could yield four wheelbarrows. The rest of the wagons would remain intact with the goods they couldn't carry left behind. Hopefully, next spring, someone would either be able to clear the road or at the very least bring more of their supplies forward by horseback. One wheelbarrow was made longer and narrower than the others. This would be Adeline's stretcher.

The women took the huge canvas covers and cut them into bags. Using rocks to push needles through the stiff material, they fashioned knapsacks that could hang across the backs of oxen and horses alike. On and on they worked, with only cups of water to sustain their strength. The wind whistled through the trees and more than once, they heard the ominous sound of more mud settling onto the slide, but no more rain fell that night.

Emil spent the night by Adeline's side, rubbing her hands and encouraging her. Occasionally, someone would go to the base of the slide and yell to him, reporting the progress.

Once again, Kim marveled at the bravery of the group. There was no lamenting for items being left behind. The decision of what to take was matter of fact. Whatever would help them survive went; anything else was stowed in the wagons. Everything was done in order of priority: life, survival implements, and then if there was any room, a few keepsakes.

Jack fashioned a narrow cart similar to the one for Adeline. Hannah stood beside him with the baby as he hammered nails. She insisted she could walk. Jack kept on hammering.

The children in the camp were quiet.They were supposed to be sleeping, but an occasional head would peep over the end of a wagon as they watched their parents dismantle what had been their homes on the trail. Around two in the morning, Kim went over to check on Bobby and found him sound asleep, wrapped up in quilts near the Harrington children. His thumb was stuck securely in his mouth. Kim gave his shoulder a gentle rub and went back to Marc.

She and Marc were a recognized unit now. Since all of Kim's things had been lost, she set herself to the task of making bags to hold as many of Marc's possessions as possible. His prized carpentry tools were put in one, the ham radio gear in a second, and his collections of vegetable seeds in a third. When no one was looking, he slipped some of his science textbooks into a bag and attached it to Rosie.

"I don't think she's limping much at all today," Kim told him.

"She'd better not," Marc said. "She and Bobby are going to be our family."

At the word "family"Kim felt tears well up in her eyes and before she knew it, she was crying. Marc folded her in his arms, and the two of them stood by the fire, drawing on each other's strength. Tomorrow, they would need it.

At daybreak, Marc and James set off, leading a horse with the makeshift stretcher strapped to its back. The horse resisted the strange bundle at first, but once they began walking, it followed obediently.

Mitchell was left in charge of leading the others to the point where the two trails merged on the other side of the mountain. Hopefully, by the time they got there, Marc and James would be there with Emil and Adeline.

Each family began the painful task of deciding what to take and what to leave behind. Size was one eliminating factor. Anything big like furniture obviously stayed in the wagons, but any farm tools that could possibly be strapped to an animal or wedged in a cart were important to include.

Before Marc left, he handed Kim a separate bag containing the HW-9.

"I'm not sure that we'll ever be able to use it again, but please try to take it."

Kim lashed the sack across Rosie's broad back. No one could really complain that she was taking valuable space because everything else Kim had owned – her wedding dress, dishes, books – all were at the bottom of the canyon.

****

Captain Bruce Thompson lay on his back and stared out at the white sand meeting the brilliant aquamarine water. It was this time of day when the heat from the sand made wavy lines in the air. Sometimes, Bruce thought he saw all sorts of shapes. Now, he squinted his eyes and tried to see something – perhaps one of his Navy buddies would come walking up the beach and tell him that this had all been a dream.

He glanced at his watch and then at the airplane. Time for another try at the radio. But what was the use? Walking to the plane would hurt his leg even more. Better to just lie still and stare at the water.

Chapter 19

The Columbia or Bust!

The plan was to wait for first light, but when snow began falling an hour before daybreak, the men agreed to start moving. The sun would be up by the time they reached the dangerous part of the trail. The Malbys and May Belle led the procession, pushing a cart and leading their oxen, laden with canvas sacks. One by one, the families fell into line. There was no talking and no one looked back. Kim and Bobby brought up the rear.

There seemed to be a new camraderie in the air. They had lost almost everything but gained knowledge of the commitment the others were willing to give. Nigel with his thousand dollars; the all night work party with everyone helping each other; the constant looking around to check on the women with young children. This would be their community and they were going to reach their promised land.

At noon, they met up with James and Emil and Marc pulling Adeline behind them in the makeshift stretcher. Adeline was wrapped in blankets and she even managed a smile for Kim.

"Are you in pain?" Kim asked her.

"Not so bad," Adeline said. "And just look at me. Why I'm being as lazy as a skunk, lying here."

Kim patted the woman's shoulder. Despite their run-ins with each other, she still felt affection for her substitute "trail mother."

"I bet one of the doctors in Oregon will be able to fix up your leg like new," Kim reassured her.

"Of course," Adeline said.

Marc fell in beside Kim at the end of the wagon train. The snow had not really gained in intensity and as the afternoon began, the sun peeked out through the white clouds and warmed them briefly.

"Do you think we've reached the summit yet?"Kim whispered to Marc.

"I don't know. I've looked at my maps, but without road landmarks, I'm not sure. Emil and James seem to think we'll be going down in elevation from here. That's why they're not allowing anyone to stop for a midday meal."

Kim listened to the rumbling of her stomach. She'd grown accustomed to the light-headed feeling of going without food, but she wondered how the others, especially the nursing mothers, were faring. Marc must have read her thoughts.

"Try not to think about food. We're going to eat tonight."

"Sure we are. Like what?" Kim asked.

"James and Emil discussed it when I was with them. One of the Dearborn oxen is old. We're going to kill it."

Kim looked ahead at the bony animal patiently carrying canvas packs and fought back tears.

"Oh Marc, isn't there any other way?"

"I don't think so. As you've seen, our hunting hasn't been too successful. These people need a good meal if they're going to keep on walking. We'll all divide the animal's packs to carry on our own," he said, anticipating her next question.

An hour before dusk, they stopped in a snow-covered meadow on the downside of the trail. James Dearborn, followed by Mitchell and Alexander, led the ox away from the group. Soon after, a single shot rang out. The women scrounged through the snow looking for dry wood and stoked the fire with pine needles and bits of bark. By the time the men returned carrying the skinned, gutted, and quartered dead animal, the fire was ready to cook. Using saws, the men cut the meat into smaller pieces so that it would cook faster.

The group stood around the fire and joined hands to sing a blessing of thankfulness for their evening meal. Kim and Marc carried their plates over to join Bobby who was holding a meaty rib with both hands and devouring it as fast he could. Kim sat down on the piece of canvas that had carried their cooking utensils. For fifteen minutes, not a word was spoken around the campfire as the life-giving meal was consumed. Kim closed her eyes, feeling the warmth of the food ease the pangs in her stomach.

The tents had been included in the materials selected. Their canvas might prove invaluable, both as makeshift shelters and for making items. Now, the men stretched them out, joining them together to make one long, narrow sleeping area. More canvas was laid on the damp ground and covered with quilts. The people lay down, putting small children between them.

Kim's legs and feet were numb as she stretched out with Bobby between her and Marc. She had a fleeting thought about how hard the ground was and then she was asleep. The sound of a solitary owl woke her several hours later. She sat up and looked down the row of sleeping people, their breath rising like steam in the frosty air.

"Kim," Marc whispered.

"What?"

"Are you okay?"

"Yeah, something woke me up, and then I started thinking about that guy we talked to. I wonder if he's still alive?"

"Maybe when we reach the Dalles, we can find materials to make another battery," Marc said.

"Yeah," said Kim as she rubbed her legs and turned on her side, trying to find a position that would allow her to go back to sleep.

****

"Isn't this sweet?" Karen had said to Bruce one day as she was showing him an old photo album from her grandparents. She pointed to a note her grandfather had written to her grandmother before their marriage. They hadn't been able to see each other that entire summer and wrote every day. In one of the notes, her grandfather had said, "I thought about you at 7 last night like we said. Did you feel it?"

In her Seattle apartment, Karen sat on the couch in front of the window that seemed to be her constant companion these days and thumbed through the photo album. The note from her grandfather caught her eye.

Concentrating, she shut her eyes. *I'm thinking about you darling. Do you feel it? Hang on. Hang on. Hang on.*

****

Captain Bruce Thompson woke with a start. He'd missed one radio schedule he'd set for himself; he wasn't about to miss another.

The leg seemed about the same as yesterday. He'd started bathing it in salt water, not knowing whether it would battle infection or encourage it. At least it was something to do, and right now, he sorely needed things to do. He'd always been accustomed to taking action, and being helpless was the worst part of this whole mess. If only there were something more he could… if only…

****

Kim drank a mug of hot water and ate a piece of cold beef for breakfast. As soon as everyone had taken some of the meat, the rest was wrapped in canvas and secured on the back of one of the other oxen. They broke camp and were on the trail by 8 o'clock. The sun that had been teasing them the day before came out for real, and until noon, they walked along the snow-covered trail watching the sunlight filter through the tall trees.

I should describe that in my journal, Kim thought and then she remembered that the journals were casualties as well as Thomas and her wedding dress. *Why is it that I don't feel happy about that?* Kim said to herself. *Maybe Adeline was right. Maybe I should have been faithful about writing in it every day.*

She mused about this and other ideas as they slogged their way through the snow which was turning increasingly mushy. Adeline had been so annoying with her old-fashioned ideas, but at the same time, she was a courageous lady and it was her determination and leadership that had helped the others. *The trick,* Kim concluded, *is to be able to take the best ideas from a generation and not to be bothered by the others.* She vowed to herself to remember that as she got older.

Hannah, who had been walking for part of the morning, was now sitting in the cart that Jack built. Kim made her way up the line to talk to her.

"Oh hello, Kimberly," Hannah said smiling up at her.

"Are you feeling all right?"

"Just a little weak in the legs. I think I could have kept on, but Jack said I had to rest awhile."

She turned to look up at her husband pushing the cart.

"Yes, I think that's a good idea," Kim agreed. "How's Kimberly?"

Hannah pulled back the cover over the sleeping infant in her arms so Kim could see her rosy face.

"I do believe she's gained a little weight," Hannah said, stroking the baby's thin face. "Don't you, dear?" she said to Jack.

"Yes, I certainly do," said Jack, but Kim could tell he didn't.

They walked on and on and on. By nightfall, they were deep in another valley and camped by a roaring stream where the men managed to catch some fish.

"Surf and Turf — $19.95," said Marc as he settled down beside Kim with his slab of beef and half trout on his plate.

"What was that?" asked Marissa Harrington, sitting nearby.

"Oh nothing, just nonsense," Marc said.

"You really have to watch that kind of stuff," Kim told him under her breath.

"I know, I know, but it just seems hard to believe that we're never going to be back in that era."

"I think right now, I'd settle for any time period as long as we had a roof over our heads and plenty to eat," Kim said.

It was true. The farther they walked, the less she thought about 1998 and her friends and family who lived there. When you got right down to it, existence was the same any place, any time. You just needed people to care about and the necessities of life. In the Willamette Valley they would have both.

****

Perhaps another good reason for "journaling" was to keep track of the days, Kim thought one morning a couple of days later. The last few days were a blur of footsteps, creaking of cart wheels, and soggy cold. They truly were past the summit of the mountains because the snow turned to rain and kept on with a vengeance that battered what was left of their spirits. On the third day, another of the oxen dropped dead on the trail, and they made camp on the spot so they could butcher and cook it.

There was no longer sorrow over lost animals. The road to Oregon was paved with sweat, tears, and bones. With every loss, it seemed as if the group hardened their resolve to make it to their destination.

"If we don't," said May Belle Fuller one evening, "then all of this will have been for nothing. My husband gave his life to lead us on the trail. We must reach the valley."

Every family bore the knowledge of its own personal sacrifices, and like May Belle, they kept on. The minutes rolled into hours; the hours into days. Get up, eat, begin walking. Drop in the evening, rest, get up, eat, and begin walking. On the fourth day or was it the fifth? Mitchell shouted from a bluff a hundred yards ahead of the group.

"I see it!"

Everyone who was able scrambled to his vantage point and followed his pointing finger. A river wound down below them.

"The Columbia?" asked Nigel.

"No, it's the John Day," said Emil.

Slowly, they made their way down the steep hill. The animals waded into the cold water and drank thirstily while the women set up camp.

"We'll see the Columbia soon," Emil told everyone after dinner. "I have notes brought back from a wagon train that went last year. We're getting close."

Normally, such an announcement would have brought a loud cheer, but now people leaned on each other with exhaustion and stared into the fire. Just a little more to go. Just a little more to go.

Ascending the hill the next day was almost impossible. Men and animals alike struggled to force their bodies to keep on going. The children tried gamely to keep up, but most of them wound up being placed on the backs of horses or oxen. It was only when an animal threatened to fall that they were taken off. Kim placed Bobby on Rosie, but when she began limping again, Marc took him off and carried him on his shoulders.

The side of one of Kim's boots split completely open and she watched the mud ooze in and out with every step. She imagined bathtubs and warm fires and down quilts. She drooled over the thought of apple pies and roast pork and baked potatoes. But looking at Marc beside her, tired, but still willing to carry a child, was the inspiration that gave her strength to keep on going. One foot after the other. It was as simple as that.

They reached the top of the hill and had rolling prairie for the next ten miles. They camped, and ate, and slept, and got up. They walked twelve more miles over a decent road and then... they saw it. Down below them was the Columbia River, more magnificent with its huge rocks and glistening white sandy shores than any of them could have imagined. For several minutes, they stood in awe, and then Emil began to pray aloud. The rest joined in. "Our Father, who art in Heaven..."

Chapter 20

A Spark in Time

They reached the Deschutes River three miles later and used a rope ferry to cross it. The next day they climbed the steep bluffs with great difficulty. If it hadn't been for the sight of the magnificent river below them, they might simply have collapsed. But a new energy seemed to have infused all of them and for the first time in a week, there was excited chatter at every resting place.

That night, they arrived at the Dalles Methodist Mission, and dined on succulent salmon given to them by Indians in trade for a box of beads that Carolyn Malby miraculously produced from a bag in their cart. The staff of the mission joined them with added foodstuffs and fellowship. They were used to buoying up the spirits of tired travelers, and they knew that souls needed as much encouragement as bodies. As the travelers ate together at a long wooden table, they heard stories about those who had gone before them.

"Tomorrow," said Emil formally after they had eaten and prayed. "Tomorrow, we will reach the Dalles proper. We will use some of our cash to buy necessary provisions. I understand there are boats that we can buy transport on for our women and children to Oregon City. The men will remain behind to build rafts for our animals and carts."

Emil paused before continuing.

"Once we reach the Willamette Valley, we will seek our spots to settle. It is possible that some of us will decide on one place and others on a different one. This may be our last evening together as a community."

"No," protested Marissa Harrington. "I believe we will stay together."

"On occasion yes," said Emil, "and in spirit always, but by the very nature of the different occupations we seek, we may not live close together."

He paused and looked around at the group. Marc reached out for Kim's hand and held it tightly in both of his.

"This has been a difficult journey," said Emil. "One that has caused us personal grief and great hardship. I want to say to you that I admire the strength that each of you has shown. I believe we are all stronger people now than when we left Missouri, and I believe we can use that strength to guide our lives well. May God be with each of you."

There was a moment of silence and then May Belle Fuller began singing "Amazing Grace." Every voice joined in.

****

The women and children lined up on the bank to board the flat-bottomed boat that would take their group down the Columbia to Oregon City. There were tearful good-byes between husbands and wives and promises that they would be together in a week. Everyone seemed surprised when Kim and Bobby insisted on staying behind with Marc, but no one countered their decision. When the Harringtons got on, Marissa turned to Bobby and, with a questioning look on her face, asked if he wanted to come with them. He shook his head no and clung to Kim's skirt.

Chapter 21

The Power of Water

The men stood motionless until the boat bearing their loved ones was out of sight. Then Emil turned to them. "We have a lot of work to do," he said. "We're going to need logs for the rafts."He pointed at a cut-over stand of firs which had obviously been used by earlier travelers. "We'll divide into groups of two to get the necessary trees, and then we'll all work together to build the rafts."

"Do you want me to go with you?" Mitchell asked as he sat down on the ground to rub an ankle he had twisted.

"Why don't you let me go up the river a ways and see what's up there," Marc suggested. "If it looks like there's more suitable wood, I'll come get you."

Mitchell readily agreed, happy for the rest, and Marc followed by Kim and Bobby, riding Rosie, made their way up the riverbank. It was raining again and the famous Columbia Gorge winds whipped the river into a froth of white caps. Kim shivered and pulled her cloak around her. The temptation to just stay put inside for the day was great, but since she'd insisted on staying behind to help, then help she would.

With their heads bent against the wind, the three of them, plus Rosie carrying their packs, made their way up the river bank toward the trees Marc was sure he saw in the distance. They walked on and on and when they finally reached the trees, they weren't much better than the ones they'd left.

"Let's go back," Kim suggested wearily.

"Just a little ways more. I want to see what's around that bend."

Vowing not to be a complainer, Kim gritted her teeth and walked on. They rounded the gentle curve in the river and Marc stopped.

"Well I'll be," Marc said, pointing at a speck way off in the distance. Almost looks like a grain mill."

"Marc, we can buy flour in the store," Kim protested.

"I'm not thinking about flour," he said, hurrying.

"Well then what are you thinking?"

He turned around and stared at her. She was tired and dirty and holding Bobby against her... and he felt his heart fill with love for her.

"Kim," he said gently. "I have an idea. Maybe it's a crazy one, but then as you and I have both agreed, this whole thing is crazy. Come on. Let's go see what that is. It's just a little way."

Reluctantly, Kim followed him up the river bank with Rosie, carrying Bobby, following patiently behind them. Bobby leaned forward and grasped the horse's mane with his hand and put his head down against her neck. The distance that Marc described as just "a little way" turned into quite a hike and Kim thought her feet would fall off when they finally reached the juncture of a roaring tributary pouring into the Columbia. An abandoned stone mill house with a motionless water wheel sat on the edge of the smaller waterway.

"Is anybody using it?" Kim asked.

"Doesn't look like it," Marc said, opening the door to the room inside.

A dusting of flour lay on the stone floor and cobwebs hung from the raftered ceiling. A broken belt used to attach the wheel to a smaller pulley inside lay in rotted pieces on the floor. Marc bent over to pick one up. Then he went back outside to inspect the water wheel. He pulled a metal bar loose that was locking it in place and smiled as the wheel began turning slowly in the current. He turned to Kim.

"Want to get on the air?"

"Marc Lawrence, have you gone crazy?"

But then as Marc pulled his bag of ham radio gear down from Rosie's back, Kim began to smile too.

"Are you going to do what I think you are?" she asked.

"I'm going to try. Hmmm. I've got a bar magnet in my spare parts bag, but I need a smaller electro magnet."

"The HW-9. In the headphones," Kim said excitedly.

"Now, how did you know that?"

"Remember when you were lost in the woods and were sending those weird signals. I got a catalogue that showed drawings of that model, hoping I'd understand whatever it was you were trying to do."

Marc was already dismantling one of the earphones to his HW-9. Bobby squatted down, watching the water splash as the water wheel turned.

"Hey, Bobby, could you drag that other bag over here – the one with my carpenter tools."

Bobby let the bag down from Rosie with a clunk and pulled it over to Marc who immediately dumped its contents on the ground.

"Here's what we want," he said holding up a bar magnet. "And of course, super glue – never leave home without it," he said grabbing a tube from the bottom of his survival kit.

Kim and Bobby followed him into the mill house to watch as he glued the magnet to the end of the shaft extending through the pulley. Then he attached the electro magnet from the headphone to a stake and pushed it into the ground beneath the pulley. He rotated the pulley by hand and looked pleased to see that the bar magnet on the shaft barely missed the smaller magnet on the stake with each rotation.

"Now, we need something to use for a belt."

Marc laughed as both his and Kim's eyes looked out the door at Rosie, her head bent down grazing with her reins dragging the ground.

"She's so good, she doesn't need them anyway," Kim said as she went outside to slip the long leather strap from over the horse's head.

Marc fastened the ends together with a rivet, making a circle of the leather. He held it up to the hub and nodded with satisfaction that the width of the strap would fit. He replaced the

164

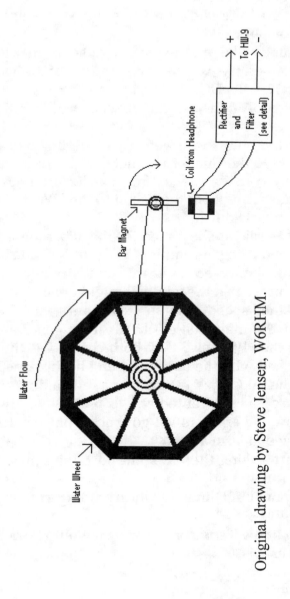

Original drawing by Steve Jensen, W6RHM.

165

bar in the water wheel, stopping it. Kim was already rummaging through electronic parts.

"Here you go," she said, spreading out Marc's spare transceiver parts on a rock.

Kim watched as he put the parts together to make a circuit that would convert the AC pulses coming out of the headphone coil unit into 12 volts DC.

"I bet you get A's on your lab projects in electronics," Kim said.

Marc was too busy to answer. There were two headphone wires attached to the smaller magnet and he connected those with his newly-constructed circuit. Next, he fastened the positive and minus wires from the circuit to the HW-9.

"Ready?" he asked Kim.

"Ready," she said as she pulled the metal bar loose from the water wheel and it began spinning. The pulley inside the house began turning at an even faster rate and Kim and Marc held their breath, afraid that the rein-belt might break. It didn't and the pulley gained speed, spinning faster and faster. With each near miss of the magnets, electricity was generated. Marc switched on the HW-9 and they both cheered as the dials lit up. Kim listened with the one remaining headphone.

"Static," she said. They listened for a few minutes that way and then Marc leaned over to her.

"You know the answers we got back from the pilot were always delayed at least a day."

"So you are saying there is some sort of a time warp factor involved," Kim said.

"I don't know, but I think it's worth sending a message about that pilot."

"We don't know if someone hearing it would be in the same year, whatever it is."

"So what do you suggest?"

Kim shrugged.

"That we send the message. And then let's send one about ourselves."

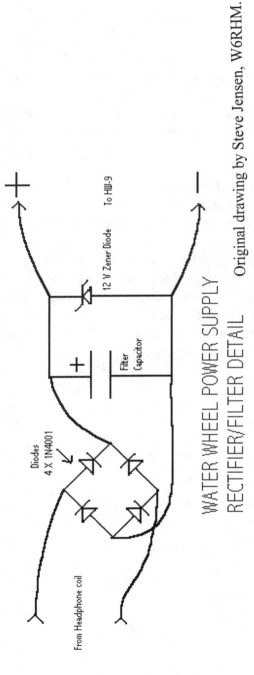

WATER WHEEL POWER SUPPLY
RECTIFIER/FILTER DETAIL   Original drawing by Steve Jensen, W6RHM.

Marc's headphone electromagnet will generate alternating polarity voltage pulses as the north and south ends of the rotating magnet pass by. The HW-9 requires +12V DC. The 4 diodes are arranged in such a fashion that the negative pulses coming out of the headphone coil will be "inverted" so they come out as positive pulses. The positive pulses will feed straight through. The capacitor stores charge so that between the pulses, the HW-9 draws power from the capacitor, and during the pulses, the capacitor is recharged. This is called a "ripple filter." The 12V zener diode limits the output voltage to a maximum value of 12 Volts DC so as to avoid damage to the HW-9 that might occur if the water wheel spins too fast and the voltage would otherwise exceed 12 Volts.

167

"Okay," Marc agreed.

Marc nodded and grabbed the code key. *SOS to any station listening,* he sent. *If you're copying this signal, there is an American Navy pilot down on a Pacific Island at approximately 15.1N Lat. And 146 E. Long. His name is Captain Bruce Thompson. Please search for him.*

Marc sent the message three times and then Kim listened on the earphones for a reply. She shook her head. Nothing. Marc handed the code key to Kim and took the earphones from her.

"Okay your turn... I mean our turn."

Kim thought a minute and then began sending. *We are stranded in the Dalles, Oregon in 1845 and we need help. This is KA7SJP and KA7ITR.*

She clenched her fingers around the key to send the message again, but turned it loose as a huge spark jumped from the transmitter to her hand. Bobby screamed as the belt on the water wheel begin spinning faster and faster, sending a shower of sparks around the room, bouncing from wall to wall. Kim clutched her head and dropped to the floor.

Chapter 22

"Now?"

C lub President Ron Mathis was the first to reach the stage when the spark gap transmitter erupted in an electrical firestorm. Despite the danger to himself, he grabbed the feet of Marc and dragged him a distance away. Two other members removed Kim and Bobby at the same time. As concerned friends bent over the unconscious bodies of the trio, they flinched as the transmitter exploded into flame, engulfing the table and the bags underneath. By the time the fire department arrived a few minutes later, all that was left were ashes and a melted piece of tone wheel from the spark transmitter.

Kim regained consciousness in the ambulance, groaning.

"Stop the water," she said. "It's exploding."

"It's okay, now," a paramedic reassured her. "You're all okay, now."

In a daze, she watched as emergency room personnel examined her and Marc and Bobby, shaking their heads in disbelief that they hadn't suffered any harm. Within an hour, all three of them were fully conscious and asking for hamburgers and milk shakes. The doctors insisted that they stay overnight for observation.

The next evening, all three were discharged to the care of their parents. As Kim drove home with her mother and father, looking out at the familiar streets of Salem, the paramedic's phrase rang through her head once more. *It's okay, now.* The question was *when was now?* She thought about trying to explain what had happened to her parents, but she couldn't find the words to even begin. And the next morning, the whole thing seemed fuzzy in her mind.

On Tuesday, before she went back to college, she phoned Bobby's parents and was relieved to hear that he had returned to kindergarten and was feeling fine. Kim's mother drove her to Corvallis and let her out at the dorm.

"Now you try to get some extra rest, dear. You've had a big shock to your system."

"I will, Mom. Don't worry."

Kim kissed her mother good-bye and hurried into the dorm. The "electrocution" had made the local papers, and Kim was greeted by friends who were anxious to see how she was. She assured them all that she was fine and tried to brush the whole thing off as a non-event. She returned to her classes that afternoon. When she came out of zoology lab, Marc was waiting for her. With his clean-shaven face and fresh jeans and sweatshirt, she almost didn't recognize him.

"Hi," he said.

"Hi," Kim said, almost shyly, wondering how you were supposed to greet someone you had been destined to marry in another time period.

"Are you feeling okay?" he asked.

"Super duper," she said.

"How about a cup of coffee before dinner?" he asked.

"I'd rather have a hamburger," she said. "I'm still hungry."

"Me too," laughed Marc. "It's like I can't eat enough."

Over hamburgers and fries, they began to talk quietly about what happened.

"Guess where I spent the morning?" Marc said.

"Where?"

"In the Oregon history section of the library."

"And?"

"I couldn't find a single reference to the wagon train. Oh, there are lots of Harringtons and Fullers and Simmons, etc. who settled in Oregon, but I couldn't find a specific mention of a group in 1845 who barely made it."

"Oh," Kim said, looking down at her empty plate. "Well you know they're not all in history books. I suppose we'd have to start searching the genealogy of each family and then interview people for possible diaries they might have."

"Do you really want to do that?"

"No," said Kim thoughtfully. "I'm not sure why this all happened or if it did, but being there was very real for me, and the experiences changed my life."

"Me too," said Marc.

"You don't think we imagined it, do you?"

He shook his head and spoke quietly so no one at other tables could hear them.

"I looked up W7DL on the data base."

"Was he there?"

"Yup. Lives in Seattle."

"The call could have been re-assigned," Kim said.

"Nope. Bruce Thompson. Born 1918. Got his license in 1930."

"Wow," Kim said. "And he was a Navy pilot, he told us."

Kim looked at Marc.

"World War II," he said quietly. "I want to go meet him," Marc said.

"We can't."

"Why not?"

"Because," Kim said and then paused to think. "Because first of all, if this didn't happen and we somehow just shared a hallucination, then the guy would think we were crazy."

"But if it did happen?" Marc questioned.

"Then we really can't," Kim said. "How would we explain talking to him in the 1940's and still being young? And if we did tell him our story and he told other people, we'd be declared nut cases or investigated by the F.B.I. or somebody. Maybe they'd lock us up in cages or want to dissect us or something."

"You watch too many movies," Marc laughed.

"Maybe you don't watch enough," Kim countered.

"Hey, easy. Is that any way to talk to the man you were supposed to marry?"

Kim smiled and looked down again.

"So you remember that part of it too?'

"Of course I do," Marc said, reaching for her hand. "The promises about building you a home, how sad you were when your wedding dress was destroyed... the whole bit."

Kim looked up at him.

"You know, there's no reason, why that can't all come true someday."

"Do you mean that?"

"Of course, I mean that." He lowered his voice and affected a Missouri twang similar to the one he'd had growing up in the 1840's. "But I won't marry you until I build you a home in Oregon. Isn't that what I said? Until I build us a future?"

"That was exactly what you said."

****

On Saturday, they drove to Seattle. Marc said he'd come up with a plan and he explained it to Kim on the way.

"Look, I have to know. That's all there is to it. If we were both just dreaming courtesy of extra electricity, then so be it, but if we weren't, I want to know."

"You called him?" Kim asked.

"Yes, I said we were writing a report on Northwest Amateur Radio operators who served in World War II."

"And he bought that?"

"Sure. He said he'd be glad to have company... that he'd been really lonely since his wife died last year."

"Did you tell him we were hams?" Kim asked.

"No, and I'd rather not, if we can get away with it. He'd want to know our calls."

"I'm not a good liar, Marc."

"We won't lie. We'll just say we're studying for the test now. That's the truth too. We both want to upgrade."

"Okay," Kim agreed reluctantly.

They practiced the questions they were going to ask him.

Even so, Kim felt nervous when they arrived at Pinewood Street in Seattle just after noon. Bruce Thompson's house was at the end of the tree-lined street. The last rose blossoms from an immacutalely-kept garden were fluttering to the ground as the two of them walked up the stone path to the door. Bruce answered on the first knock.

White-haired, slightly stooped, he still carried himself with military dignity and was dressed in khaki slacks and a green wool sweater. He opened the door wide and greeted them warmly.

"I've been expecting you all morning. Come on in."

They followed him into a cedar-paneled family room and sat down in front of a crackling fire in the brick fireplace.

"So you're from OSU, right?"

"Yes," said Marc.

"Marc and Kim, right?"

"Yes," Kim said as Bruce looked at her as though he was analyzing her very being.

"The report's for a history class," Kim said, hoping he wouldn't say that he wanted to see a copy of it when they were done. "We just thought that interviewing ham radio operators who had served during the war might be an interesting subject."

"Why is that?"

"Well," began Marc. "We're both studying for ham radio tests ourselves – we've become quite interested in the hobby and we just decided to look up some of its history."

Kim felt her heart beating fast, glad that she didn't have to answer that question.

"Well, I can tell you this," said Bruce Thompson, "if it weren't for Amateur Radio, I wouldn't be alive today."

"Really?" said Marc.

Chills ran up Kim's spine as the captain began telling his story.

"In June of 1944, I had to crash land my Hellcat on a little island in the Pacific. I was hurt – broke my leg and ankle," he said, rubbing his shin, "but the worst part is that none of the searchers found me. I was stuck out there for almost three weeks. By that time, I was pretty sick. Blood poisoning, I guess they called it."

"Who found you?" Kim asked.

"The Navy sent a special aerial squadron to look for me. It seems they had assumed I was dead. You see, I had tried to contact them by radio but didn't have any luck. Then one day, I heard someone on the ham radio bands. I was really surprised since no one was supposed to be on with the blackout."

Kim and Marc sat on the edge of their seats as the man continued.

"Actually, I heard two people on two different days. The strangest part was that there seemed to be some sort of a delay in our hearing each other. I'd send a message one day and get an answer the next. Strange, strange," he said, shaking his head. "They both had KA something calls which of course weren't valid U.S. calls then. I just assumed they were bogus so that if anyone heard them, they wouldn't be caught. And to tell you the truth, they didn't seem that bright. One of them asked me what the date was."

Kim hoped her cheeks weren't growing red. She could feel the sweat on her palms, but Marc seemed to be cool about the whole thing.

"These hams... what happened?"

"I don't really know. Apparently, two weeks after I heard them, one of them transmitted again and gave my location and told any station listening to contact the Navy. Someone in Astoria heard that transmission and called the Coast Guard. And here I am today, " said Bruce smiling at both of them.

"That's quite a story," said Kim.

"It's a true one," said Bruce. "I just wish that I could have thanked whoever it was in person. Actually, I was quite concerned about them because about an hour after the message about me was picked up, there was another one from these folks saying they were in trouble in the Dalles."

174

Kim and Marc sat silently, just staring at Bruce.

"Aren't you going to write any of that down?" asked Bruce, motioning toward their empty pads of paper.

"I think we'll remember it," said Kim.

They visited for another hour or so and drank hot cups of tea. Bruce showed them photos of his wife, Karen, and their two sons and five grandchildren. About two, Marc stood up.

"I guess we'd better go," he said. "It's a long drive back to Corvallis."

"Well I hate to see you folks go," Bruce said. "This has been a real treat."

"We've enjoyed it too," said Kim.

He walked with them to the door and shook their hands. Kim and Marc stepped out on the walkway.

"Thanks for telling us about what happened."

"My pleasure," said Captain Bruce Thompson. "I've been waiting a long time to share that story."

They were halfway down the walk when he called out to them.

"KA7ITR."

Instinctively, Marc whirled around.

"KA7ITR," the captain repeated. "That's what the call of one of them was. I just remembered it."

"Oh," Marc said.

The captain's blue eyes focused on Marc and Kim.

"And like I said, I really wanted to tell those folks thank you."

"I'm sure they know you're grateful," said Marc.

"I'm sure they do too," said the captain.

"Well good-bye again," said Kim.

"Goodbye," said the captain. "You two come back any time."

He smiled at them as he repeated it.

"Any time at all."

Author's Note

When I started talking to students a year ago about the possibility of writing a time travel story, their enthusiastic response encouraged me to create this latest adventure of Kim and Marc. Whether you're a fan of science fiction or not, I hope you have enjoyed their excursion into the past.

By reading the journals of Oregon pioneers, I have learned a great deal about the courage and daring, and yes, even the mistakes, that accompanied them on their westward trek. The important thing was that they never gave up. The same can be said for pioneers in all fields. Early experiments in electricity have given us the wonderful technological supermarket of goods we enjoy today including our ham radio transceivers. Early experiments in medicine have given us antibiotics and life-saving procedures. For a few weeks, Kim and Marc were able to live in a time when the wonders we take for granted today were just ideas.

What lies ahead for 21st Century pioneers? All things are possible. As long as man continues to have courage, the adventure will continue.

73, *Cynthia Wall* KA7ITT

I would like to thank the following people for their help.
Wil Claus, W7DL
John Herbert
Steve Jensen, W6RHM
Dick and Mary Lutz
Jim Maxwell, W6CF
Hollie Molesworth, KA7SJP
Richard Ritterband, AA6BC
Bob Wall
Dave Wall
Michael Wall, KA7ITR